She'd liked working with him.

He took his job seriously. They all did. It was her dream job, and not once had she regretted returning home. But now that Nick had landed on her workplace doorstep, that might change everything.

Only if I let him.

True. She was in charge of her own destiny, something she'd repeatedly told herself over the years dealing with bullies. While Nick wasn't a bully, he did seem to hold sway over her emotions, and that needed dealing with sooner than later. He was already changing her, in that she did want to get to know him better and to have fun. Like between the sheets again? It had been incredible before.

He was still watching her.

"I'm not trying to cause trouble, Leesa. I know I've landed on your patch. We can work together without that brief fling causing trouble between us."

"Of course we can." She went for honesty. "I enjoyed today. You're a great doctor, and good with patients." *I was relaxed when I wasn't recalling how your hands felt on my body.*

Dear Reader,

Nick has lost everyone special to him, so believing he's lovable and able to risk his heart yet again is nigh on impossible. Yet when he meets Leesa, everything changes—except the caution wrapped around his heart.

For Leesa, who's been bullied by her ex-husband and a boss, it's all about being strong for herself and not letting another man try to take over her life. But when she falls for Nick, it's hard and deep, and she's willing to take another chance on love—if only Nick was, too.

Enjoy reading how these two resolve their differences to find their HEA.

All the best,

Sue MacKay

PARAMEDIC'S FLING TO FOREVER

SUE MACKAY

MEDICAL ROMANCE

Harlequin®
MEDICAL ROMANCE

Recycling programs for this product may not exist in your area.

ISBN-13: 978-1-335-94249-4

Paramedic's Fling to Forever

Copyright © 2024 by Sue MacKay

Harlequin Enterprises ULC
22 Adelaide St. West, 41st Floor
Toronto, Ontario M5H 4E3, Canada
www.Harlequin.com

Printed in U.S.A.

Sue MacKay lives with her husband in New Zealand's beautiful Marlborough Sounds, with the water on her doorstep and the birds and the trees at her back door. It is the perfect setting to indulge her passions of entertaining friends by cooking them sumptuous meals, drinking fabulous wine, going for hill walks or kayaking around the bay—and, of course, writing stories.

Books by Sue MacKay

Harlequin Medical Romance

Queenstown Search & Rescue

Captivated by Her Runaway Doc
A Single Dad to Rescue Her
From Best Friends to I Do?

The GP's Secret Baby Wish
Their Second Chance in ER
Fling with Her Long-Lost Surgeon
Stranded with the Paramedic
Single Mom's New Year Wish
Brought Together by a Pup
Fake Fiancée to Forever?
Resisting the Pregnant Pediatrician
Marriage Reunion with the Island Doc

Visit the Author Profile page
at Harlequin.com for more titles.

To Auntie Joc. Thank you for all the wonderful memories. Love, Susan.

PROLOGUE

'HI. MIND IF I sit here?'

Leesa Bennett looked up at the guy standing in front of her with a beer in his hand and nodded. 'Sure.'

She was hardly going to say no when this was a communal party, in the park next to the apartment block where she lived. Though only for one more week before she was on the road heading north, home to Cairns. Back to her family and the world she'd missed ever since coming to Brisbane with her ex. If only she had known what awaited her here, she'd never have packed one bag, let alone all her belongings, to move south.

'Thanks.' The newcomer's voice was deep and husky, and a dark beard covered his lower face. A sexy combination, if ever she'd seen one.

Gasping, she swallowed a large mouthful of gin from her can and promptly coughed. Sexy? Definitely. But she didn't usually get in a twist about a hot-looking man. Didn't get in a twist at all these days, especially about men. One too many had made her life hell to be letting any others close.

'Easy.' A steady hand patted her back.

'Thanks.'

She sat up straighter and took a smaller sip. The guy wasn't familiar to her, but then she didn't know everyone living in the block or attending the barbecue, which had been organised by the apartment tenants' committee. He hadn't been helping the other men cooking the steaks and sausages, but not all the men had. There wouldn't have been room.

'Did you have some food?' she asked.

'No.'

Not a great talker then. Suited her. She was feeling low and not in the mood for idle chatter, especially with a stranger. Even a sexy one.

There she went again. Sexy. Showed how long it was since she'd let her hair down and had some fun with a guy. Was it time to do so?

Now that she was finally leaving Brisbane it was dawning on her how she was closing a chapter of her life. A chapter that had been tough and full of hurt and that she was ready to leave behind. Still, she felt sad. The earlier dreams she'd had, of a wonderful marriage and a new life in an exciting city, had all turned into a nightmare.

She'd left her husband after accepting that he would never stop bullying her, even when she stood up to him. After being bullied at school, she knew there was only one way to go with Connor and that was to leave him. He'd get worse as time went on, not better. He'd tried to deny her a divorce, saying they had too much to lose and that he loved her to the end of the earth and back. So why demand she make the bed with hospital folds like his mother used to, and expect roast lamb for dinner every Tuesday, and make her wash the car on Saturday mornings even if she had to go to work? The list went on, but she'd put it behind her when she left him.

Only to end up working with another bully who thought he could tell all the female staff at the ambulance base what to do and when. Not the men. Oh, no, they were free to sit back and let the women clean the ambulances and restock everything. Not that any of them did, but that wasn't the point. That prat hadn't counted on her having already learned how to deal with someone like him. When he'd sacked her for standing up to him, she'd fought her dismissal with management and won, because they'd heard rumours about the man's attitude. After that she went on to stick up for the others he bullied and, in the end, he was the one to leave with his tail firmly between his legs.

Despite everything that had gone down over the last two years, in some ways she was sorry to be moving away. Brisbane was a great place to live, despite the feeling something was missing for her. She did have a great job lined up with the Flying Health Care service in Cairns, and spending more time with her family was high on her priority list, especially now her mother had been diagnosed with early-stage Parkinson's. Her grandmother's house was waiting for her, as Gran had moved into a retirement village and didn't want the house sold yet.

'You live in one of the apartments?' her companion asked.

'I do. A one-bedroom unit. It's great.' She watched some of the women dancing on the lawn to the music belting out from speakers hanging from trees. 'But I'm moving on in a few days, going back home to Cairns where my family are.'

'I've just moved up here.'

'So, you're not on holiday then?' She didn't really need to know, but might as well keep the conversation ticking over and put her glum thoughts behind her.

He shook his head. 'No, I'm spending a couple of nights with a mate while I find somewhere permanent.' He drained his beer. 'I'm starting a new job in a couple of weeks.'

So, he could do talking when he chose. 'Doing what?'

'I'm a doctor. Going to work with the emergency service.'

'Right.' Small world. She decided not to mention she'd finished working in the same area one day ago. Her reputation went before her and, while most people thought she was great for helping her work mates face up to that prat, there were a few who thought she was nothing more than a troublemaker. 'Think I'll get another drink. Can I get you something?'

He stood up. 'I'll come with you.'

Not the answer she'd expected. He seemed reticent about talking too much, but he had sat with her so it could be he knew no one and wanted some company. She understood that. After all that had gone down over the last two years, she was cautious about who she talked to. People always took sides even when they didn't know the whole story.

That had been a major lesson she'd learned in all the turmoil. She used to be a slow learner, too willing to trust people even after being bullied at school. She hadn't recognised the signs when she married Connor. But she knew better now and was not going to hand over her heart so readily ever again, if at all.

'Grab some food while we're at it,' Leesa suggested.

'No, thanks.'

'Not into barbecues?'

Who wasn't? They were an Ozzie tradition.

His sigh hung between them. 'I had a big lunch.'

Okay, she'd shut up now. She might be feeling flat, but this was a party, and keeping quiet wasn't really her thing—not for long periods anyway. Digging into her chilly bin she grabbed another gin and popped the top.

'Who's your friend that lives here?' So she didn't know when to shut up after all. No surprise there.

At least he replied with a small smile, giving her a name she didn't recognise. 'Logan Brand. We met in med school.'

'I don't know if my apartment has been rented out yet, if you're interested. I'm on the tenth floor,' she added.

'I'll think about it.'

Taking a mouthful of her drink, she watched those who were dancing on the lawn and decided to join them. 'Into dancing by any chance?'

His eyes widened and he actually laughed. 'Yes, I am. Let's give it a whirl.' Without waiting for a reply, he took her arm and led her over to where people were shaking and wiggling, laughing uproariously about who knew what.

Leesa struggled to ignore the hot sensations his hand caused on her arm. Not only did he look sexy, he had a touch that sent her off balance. Blimey. So much for a quiet night. She was about to wiggle her ass in front of this guy. Best she went and sat down again.

Except they were already in the midst of the crowd and being jostled left and right. Her new friend's hand was now on her waist, making sure she didn't get nudged too far away from him. Moving in time to the music, she drank in the sight before her. Her companion might be quiet, but did he have the moves or what? Those firm hips swung all over the place, keeping a perfect rhythm to the music, while his feet were light on the ground and his upper body was a sight she couldn't ignore. She did try, but, hey, some things weren't meant to happen.

Settle, girl. You're leaving town in five days.

Yes, so why not have some no-strings fun with a sexy man?

Because she didn't usually hook up for one-night stands. That was why. Would it hurt to stretch the boundaries for once? Taking in the sight before her, it was hard to come up with an answer to that. Other than, 'Yes, go for it.'

'Why are you smiling so much?' he asked.

'Because I'm happy.' It was true. She really was. Gone was the sadness over this being the end of another phase of her life. Suddenly she felt there were opportunities out there she hadn't considered. Like letting go of her hang up over trusting a man not to demand her utmost attention all the time. She was probably overreacting because this man was hot, but did it matter? Tomorrow was another day. Tonight was to be enjoyed now. 'Nothing better than dancing.'

Nothing she was mentioning at any rate. He'd probably run away faster than a greyhound on the track. Even if he didn't, the last thing she wanted was him knowing what was going on in her mind, and other parts of her body.

He took her hand and whirled them around. 'Couldn't agree more.'

Thankfully he'd be thinking about the dancing and would have no idea of the thoughts racing through her head. Fingers crossed.

Suddenly the music stopped mid-song. 'That's it, folks. It's midnight and as you know the council forbids music to be played in their parks after that.'

Leesa blinked. 'Where'd the time go?' She'd have sworn they had at least another hour to go. Went to show how much fun she'd been having dancing with Dr Sexy. What was his name? Did it matter? Dr Sexy suited him better than any other name she could come up with.

'Feel like another drink before you head upstairs?' he asked.

'Sounds good to me.' She had nothing important on in the morning so it didn't matter if she slept in.

'I'll get your chilly bin.' He sauntered across the grass, looking more at ease than when he'd first sat down beside her a couple of hours back.

Had she made him feel comfortable? Or had he just got over whatever had been keeping him quiet? Whatever. She liked him. She knew nothing about him, but that didn't matter. She was out of here on Wednesday and wouldn't be looking back, no matter what.

'Here you go.' He handed over a can and sat down beside her on the park bench, a beer in hand.

'Thanks.' She popped the can. 'Is your mate still here?'

'He and his girlfriend headed away to his apartment a little while go. I'm giving them some time alone.'

'You can come and checkout the apartment I'm in if you like.' *This late at night? Why not?*

He studied her intently. 'You sure? You don't know me.'

'You dance okay.' After dancing with him she really wanted to have some more fun.

A grin appeared. 'Then yes, I'll take a look at your place. I like the location and I know from my mate's apartment the place's kept in good shape.' So far, he was keeping to the script.

She could do that too. 'I've had no complaints in the time I've been here.'

'Which is how long?' He'd got a whole lot chattier. Must've liked her dance moves too.

When I left Connor.

'Over a year, give or take.' She stood up, suddenly restless. She wasn't into talking about her past. Plus, this man was attractive beyond reason, making it hard not to reach out and tuck herself into that amazing chest. Which would really have him thinking she was a fruit loop. Or a loose woman. Something she most definitely was not, but for some reason tonight she was ready to make the most of whatever this man had to offer. 'Let's go.'

'Give me your chilly bin.' He took it without waiting for an answer.

'Thank you.' Not that she'd have turned down his offer, even if the bin weighed less than a banana. It was nice being treated so well for a change. She had let her barriers down a little. Dr Sexy had been nothing but decent all evening. Throw in the growing need to have some me-time and he was getting more attractive by the minute.

In the crowded elevator Leesa found herself pressed firmly against his hard muscular body, liking every moment. His long body was a good fit. It wasn't often she felt comfortable with her height, but for once she did. Being taller than all the other girls at school had been another reason kids teased her. Apparently, girls were supposed to be slim and medium height. It had got better out in the adult world, but the sense of being different hadn't quite left her, especially when her ex had told her that she should be grateful he found her attractive.

As the lift became less packed at each floor Dr Sexy didn't move away, instead he stayed right beside her with his hand touching hers without actually holding it.

'Level ten,' intoned the metallic speaker.

They stepped out into the corridor. Without thinking she took her companion's hand, and didn't let go. His warmth felt so good she didn't care if this was a suggestive move. Which, come to think of it, it was. The realisation didn't change a thing. She couldn't remember ever feeling so relaxed but so fired up, her body melting on the inside for the first time in for ever. 'This way. My apartment's on the front of the building.'

He didn't drop her hand until they reached her door. Delving into her pocket for the key, she shivered. What was she doing? Showing this guy the apartment, or looking for that fun she wanted? Leesa's breathing stalled. He was watching her with the same need reflected in his deep blue eyes. Did she let him in? Or was this the opportunity to come to her senses and say goodnight?

'I can go if you'd prefer.'

His face was open and honest. The light beard covering his chin made her palms itch. Desire spiralled throughout her. Elbowing the door open she stepped inside. 'Come in.'

He followed her inside and closed the door quietly. Turning to face her, he said with a crooked smile that added to his sexiness, 'We haven't introduced ourselves. My name is Nick.'

Funny how they hadn't got around to mentioning names before. 'Leesa.' A lot of thumping was going on in her chest as she fell into those eyes. Beautiful. They stirred up her desire so it was now an eddy whirling from her mouth to her toes.

The chilly bin hit the floor with a soft thump as Nick reached for her, his hands on her shoulders pulling her close to that sensational body.

Slipping her arms around his neck she pressed into him, her breasts hard against his expansive chest, making her nipples tight as she lifted her mouth to his.

His sex was hard against her lower abdomen, telling her there was no doubt why he'd come up to her apartment. He wanted a first-hand view of the bedroom.

A view she was all too happy to share. But only when she'd had her fill of his kisses. He kissed like there was no tomorrow, devouring her while at the same time tender and teasing. She held him tighter, pushed closer and kissed him in return, giving way to the need taking over, going with him all the way until finally she had to have more.

Pulling back, she grabbed his hand. 'Come on.' Heading to her bedroom, she rued the fact she had to wait even seconds to get down and naked, but the condoms were in her bathroom cabinet in the ensuite. 'I need to get protection.'

'I've got some,' Nick told her.

'Cool.' A prepared man. She lifted her t-shirt over her head and dropped it on the floor. 'Then there's nothing to wait for.'

'You are in a hurry.'

She blinked. Did she sound too eager, when she rarely did something like this? 'Sorry.' Hello? Sounding like the girl who tried to placate people to keep them onside.

'Don't be.' Perfect answer. Nick touched her face so softly her eyes moistened. He really was special.

Better not let him get to her more than he already had. 'I'm not usually so fast to get this close to someone,' she whispered.

'Relax, Leesa. I'm not either. If you want to change your mind that's okay.'

'Hell no.' She was grinning like crazy. He really was awesome. She wasn't talking any more. His lips were soft as she kissed him. But not for long. Within moments he was returning her kiss with a depth that would've turned her on if she wasn't already wound up so tight—she was about to spring apart.

Somehow, they ended up naked on the bed, unable to keep their hands to themselves. Drinking in the sight of Nick's body she spread her fingers over his chest, his hips, his thighs and onto the throbbing erection teasing her, begging her to let him in.

All the while Nick's fingers were working magic on her heavy breasts, tormenting her with soft caresses, heating her already overheated skin, making her head spin. She wanted him. Now. But she didn't want him to stop touching her breasts.

Then his fingers walked lightly down her body to where her pulse was throbbing so hard the whole street could probably hear. He touched, ran his finger over her sex. Almost immediately she was coming. Her whole body quivered with the explosion of desire. 'Nick, now. Please,' she begged.

When he slid inside, tears spilt down the sides of her face. This was awesome. More than awesome. There was no word to explain the out-of-this-world sensations filling her from scalp to toes. Wrapping her legs around him she hung on for the ride, loving when he pushed into her, holding her breath when he pulled back. Then she rocked as she shattered.

Nick stood looking down at the woman who'd shared her bed and herself with him. Leesa. A lovely name to suit a lovely lady. She was special.

Sure, it had been one of those nights where a few drinks and sensational dancing had played a part in them getting together. But there'd been something more about her that attracted him. She was nothing like his usual one-night stands. She hadn't pushed him for any info, she'd taken what he'd said in reply to her questions and let him be. She was friendly without going over the top— until they fell into her bed and then there was no holding back.

He smiled widely. Then stopped. Unbelievable how a few hours with Leesa made him wonder if it was time to stop and question what he was doing with his life, why he was driven to keep moving on from job to job, city to city, every couple of years.

The fact his wife had waited until she'd had an abortion to tell him she'd been pregnant, and been having affairs for a while, had had him up and leaving and filing for divorce as soon as possible. But he'd always moved on from city to city, looking for something he wasn't sure he'd find.

'What about you, Leesa? When you love some-

one, is it with all you've got?' he asked silently. Because she had stirred him up, made him think about the impossible, even long for the life he'd always dreamed of again. Did that mean she could be the one to turn him around and help him settle down?

Of course, he knew the answer to that. Nothing was going to change because of an exceptional one-night stand. After his grandfather died, he'd spent most of his life alone, living with people in the welfare system who hadn't opened their hearts to him, who couldn't love him. Nothing about tonight changed that.

And yet his heart felt lighter and brought a flare of hope for something, someone, in his future. Something that hadn't happened since his marriage went west. The passion he'd known during the night could be a game changer if he was prepared to listen to his heart and not his head for once—as his mentor, Patrick Crombie, kept saying. The judge had saved his butt, and he'd always respect him for that, as well as the in-depth conversations they'd had over the years since.

But the night had been about Leesa. He would love more than one hot night with her. Might find more with her than only amazing sex. He shivered. What? Lower the barriers in place around his heart? Let Leesa in and risk being hurt yet again? Not likely.

But really, what was there to lose? She was heading away in a few days. They could have some fun and say goodbye at the end. Nothing unusual for him, but for once he wanted more.

Because of Leesa? Because he'd shared her bed once?

She'd been so refreshingly open, saying what she wanted without getting coy, he'd taken a second look at her. Different, for sure. But his nomadic lifestyle with few close friends hadn't made him out and out happy. If only it was as easy as stepping forward and holding out his hand to get the life he yearned for. But protecting himself had become ingrained as he'd grown up, first losing his parents, then his grandfather. He'd loved his wife, trusted her to reciprocate his love, and got that horribly wrong.

Leesa breathed heavily and rolled over onto her other side, that silky long hair spilling over the pillow.

Yes, his heart definitely felt eager for more. This wonderful woman had had his chest squeezing with something akin to love, had him thinking he might one day change his life around and find happiness. Another shiver as emotions flooded him. He wanted that so much it frightened the pants off him, despite believing he must be unlovable if his parents, grandfather and wife had left him for one reason or another.

Whatever steps he took it wouldn't be Leesa who followed him into whatever came next. She was heading away, while he'd just arrived in Brisbane.

Relief poured through him. He wouldn't be tempted to make a mistake and get hurt again. Then disappointment shoved aside the relief.

He more than liked Leesa. Way more. He had to get out of here before he gave into these warm feelings of longing—the hope of dropping this inability to settle down with someone and make love and happiness happen. He really wanted it all, and suddenly, all because he'd met this wonderful woman, he could see it just might be possible. Every thought came back to Leesa.

Time to go. Not only to reflect on what had happened in the space of a few passionate hours, and make sense of these new emotions, but to try and accept he was ready to make some changes in his life.

Moving quietly so as not to disturb her, he headed for the door, then paused. In the light thrown by the full moon coming through the window he saw a notepad and pen on the kitchen bench. He couldn't help himself. He crossed to the bench, picked up the pen and wrote.

Thank you for a wonderful night. N.

He didn't know if he was saying goodbye or setting himself up for more enjoyment.

* * *

By six o'clock that night he had his answer. Pulling up outside the apartment block he turned off the engine and got out to stare up at level ten. Leesa had run around inside his head all damned day, even when he'd been looking at available rental properties. Laughing, dancing, kissing him, opening up to him. Smiling, sometimes not smiling, just sitting beside him as they watched others dancing.

Oh, man, how she'd got to him. So much so that he had to see her. He'd knock on her door on the pretext he wanted to look around the apartment, properly this time, as a possible option to rent. The location was ideal for his upcoming job, and his mate was on hand, but that had nothing to do with why he was heading up to her floor and not stopping at level four where he was staying with Logan.

He and Leesa hadn't swapped phone numbers so he was taking a punt she'd be at home. If she wasn't he'd come back later, unless he'd managed to talk himself out of it. Which he doubted was possible.

Leesa's face split into a warm smile when she opened her door to his knock. 'Nick. I didn't expect to see you again.'

Ignoring the thumping under his ribs, he asked,

'Is it okay to take a look around the apartment to see if it suits me?'

She stepped back for him to enter, her laughter tickling him on the inside. 'Let's be honest, you never really intended to inspect the place last night.'

He would've if that was all that had been on offer, but, 'You're right.' So did that mean he'd get it right this time?

'I just ordered pizza to be delivered. Want to join me? I can add to the order.'

Just like that he relaxed some more. 'Absolutely. Seafood would be great.'

'Take a look around while I deal with that.' She already had her phone to her ear. 'It won't take you more than a minute. It's kind of small in here.'

Except it did, because he paused in the doorway of her bedroom and stared at the bed where he'd had the time of his life with Leesa. He could picture her long, slight body pressed against his, under his, over his. Her tongue on his heated skin. Her fingers touching, rubbing, making him explode with desire.

'Nick? There a problem?' Leesa called from the lounge.

'Not at all.' Not anything he was mentioning. Stepping away, he turned and poked his head into the bathroom, where everything looked fine for his needs. At the end of the day apartments were apartments, and this one was in good condition and had everything he wanted. But there were still a couple more to look at tomorrow before he made a decision.

Or was he prevaricating? Because Leesa lived here? How that mattered didn't make sense since she'd soon be gone. Yes, but it would be where she'd lived, where they'd made love, where hot memories could tease him.

Once again, she interrupted his errant thoughts. 'Want a beer?'

He should leave while he still could. She was rattling his cage a bit too much. 'Love one.'

'What do you think?' she asked when they were sitting on the narrow deck watching the world go by below.

That I'd like another night in your bed.

He took a swig from his bottle, swallowed hard. 'About what?'

'The apartment, silly. Isn't that why you're here?'

Is it?

'It's fine. I've seen a few today and have agreed to look at more tomorrow, but really, it's a no-brainer. The location is ideal, my mate's handy, and I don't have any lawns to mow.'

Her eyes had widened. 'When I first met you last night, you didn't say as much in an hour.'

Yeah, well, you didn't know me then.

Still didn't, but he was working on it, because

he couldn't walk away. They had a few days to enjoy if she was up to it, and hopefully by then he'd have worked this need out of his system. 'Like I said then, I didn't want to scare you off.'

'As if.' Her grin was wicked and winding him up fast.

'How long before those pizzas arrive?' Because eating was suddenly the last thing he wanted to do.

Her grin just got more wicked. 'Patience, man.'

'Are we on the same page?' He had to know or he'd blow a gasket.

'You mean, do I want to share my salami pizza?' Damn, her eyes were the sexiest he'd ever encountered.

'You got it in one.' The sound of a bell ringing cut through the air. 'Thank goodness,' he muttered. 'Unless you've invited the neighbours in.'

'No, just my mates from work,' she grinned. 'Relax, Nick. I'll go deal to with the delivery and then we can get down and sexy.'

He watched her walk inside, that sassy bottom making him hard just thinking about touching her. Twenty-four hours ago, he hadn't even met Leesa and now—now he wanted to fall into bed with her again and make love like there was no tomorrow. He wanted to leave his mark on her so she'd never forget him. He wanted to make more memories to hold close after she left town.

And yet he knew the old fear of being let down was lurking behind all the happy thoughts. There would be nothing to gain if he didn't take some chances, but that was a huge ask. Could he do it? Could he leave the past behind and get on with the future?

'I'd say by the look that just crossed your face we'd better eat first.' Leesa looked disappointed as she stood in front of him holding two pizzas.

On his feet in an instant, Nick took the boxes from her and placed them on the table. Then he leaned in and kissed her, lightly at first, then deeper and deeper until his head spun and Leesa was gripping him tight. He raised his head. 'Which do you want?'

She took his hand and raced to her bedroom. 'I've spent half the day thinking about this while not really expecting to see you again. I'm not going to waste any more time thinking.' She spun around in front of him, tearing her t-shirt over her head, exposing her lace-clad breasts.

He should've come up hours ago, to hell with looking at apartments. The best one in town was right here. 'Thinking's highly overrated,' he groaned before his mouth found her nipple and she bucked against him.

Wednesday morning and Leesa was up at five thirty to see Nick out the door for the last time.

She had a few last things to pack before the removal company arrived to box up the furniture and transfer it all to her gran's house in Cairns, and then she'd hit the road before the heat became unbearable. 'Thanks for some amazing nights,' she said before giving him one last kiss. A not-so-passionate kiss, since she was leaving town this morning and their fling was over.

They'd shared four incredible nights with little sleep and a lot of mind-blowing sex. How was she going to move on from that? *'Apart from the four days driving that lay ahead,'* she laughed to herself. There'd be plenty of time driving to consider her options about the future.

'Back at you,' Nick said as he returned her kiss. Stepping back, his arms dropped to his side. 'Thanks for everything, Leesa.'

'All the best with your new job.' She was filling in the air between them, wanting him to leave before she grabbed him tight and changed her mind about heading north. At the same time glad she could take in more of that honed body and beautiful face to brood over later.

'Drive safely,' he returned.

'Sure.'

'Good.'

Um… 'Bye, then.'

Nick spun away, took two steps, called over his shoulder, 'Bye, Leesa.' This time he kept walking all the way along the corridor to the lift.

Before he reached it, she was inside the apartment, closing the door and scrubbing her face with her fingers. The nights with Nick had opened her heart to really getting on with finding the life she wanted, once she got home to where her family and friends were. The new life might one day include a man she'd give her heart to and who'd love her to bits in return. Plus, children to love as well. A complete family. Yep, couldn't ask for more than that. If she was ready to try again.

At six thirty she slid into her car, buckled up and then flicked some music on—loud. Pulling out of the underground garage she glanced up at the apartment building one last time. 'See you, Nick. You're an amazing lover. I've had the most wonderful time with you.' Funny thing was they'd not talked about themselves at all. As though they both wanted to have fun without getting deep. Maybe that had been a mistake. And maybe it hadn't.

Indicating left, she turned onto the street and began the long haul home. All the way Nick stayed with her, reminding her there were decent men out there and that she only had to step up and be herself and she'd find one of them.

Sure you haven't already?

Unfortunately, the music couldn't get any louder to block out that annoying voice.

CHAPTER ONE

Fourteen months later

NICK TILTED HIS head and slid the shaver down his neck. Day one of another new job. How many jobs would he have held by the time retirement age came around? His hand pulled the razor down a second time, pausing as he stared at himself in the mirror.

He was tired of always moving on.

His eyes widened as the truth struck. He was? A truth he'd been denying since those wonderful nights in Leesa's bed. No, he hadn't forgotten her, no matter how hard he'd tried.

After rinsing the shaver, he made another clean line on his neck. Yes, he was ready to make some changes. The judge had been right there. It was time to settle in one place, and stay on in a job he enjoyed for more than a couple of years.

Since Patrick, as he now called the judge, had had a serious cancer scare a few months back, he'd become more persistent that Nick should stop wandering the country and follow his dreams of love and family. To see this strong man, who Nick had always thought the world of, looking so lethargic and ill had been such a shock. It'd woken Nick up in a hurry to the fact that no one knew what was around the corner, and that dreams should be followed, not avoided.

But did that include finding a woman he could love? Yeah, well, that requisite had been high on the list of reasons not to settle, because no one ever stayed with him for long, though there were no rules saying he had to fall in love to put down roots. Except he'd love to have a child and raise him or her, giving them all he could to make their life wonderful. Not like the life he'd had growing up in the welfare system after his grandfather died, but a life full of love and understanding, support and care.

The one man who'd understood him enough to give him a second chance, the reason why he was now a doctor and starting work today at Flying Health Care, had been Patrick. Judge Crombie could've sent him to an institution when he'd been caught stealing a car because he wanted to learn to drive, but had instead handed him some strong words of advice. 'Pull your head in, stop being an idiot and start behaving, or you are going to ruin your life for ever.'

Nick had always believed that Patrick had seen

something in him that no one else had. If not for him who knew where he'd be now. Nick shook away the memory of being a hothead to get attention. No point looking back. His appalling behaviour had actually put him on the right path, something he'd be grateful for for ever, but that didn't make him ready to risk his heart by falling in love and believing he'd be loved in return. It didn't happen to him. His previous attempt had proven that, and he wasn't stupid enough to believe he'd get it right next time.

The fire alarm shrieked. And kept on shrieking.

'Great.' Nick dropped his shaver and hauled on his shorts. Probably a false alarm, but he'd better play safe or someone would have to come looking for him. He tugged a t-shirt over his head, snatched his wallet and keys from the bench, ran to the door and swung it open.

The smell of smoke struck him. This was real. Supressing a shudder, he slammed the door shut and joined the crowd racing to the stairwell, including the neighbours he'd met briefly last night—two parents who were tightly gripping their children's hands.

'Can I take your daughter?' he asked his neighbour who had a wee girl clinging to her hand while her husband held the hands of two kids a bit older.

'You'd be a champ.' The woman shoved a child in his direction. 'Cally, this is Nick. Please hold Nick's hand tight and do what he says.'

No one stopped as hands were swapped. 'Cally, is it okay if I carry you?' Nick asked as lightly as he could. Walking down the stairs would be slow for the small girl, nor would it be safe in the panicked crowd.

'Yes.'

'Thanks, Nick,' Cameron looked over his shoulder as Nick swept the tiny five-year-old up and out of the way of people intent on getting down the stairs ASAP. 'Really appreciate it.'

Like anyone wouldn't do the same. 'No problem.' He concentrated on the stairs along with the pushing and shoving going on. It wasn't easy avoiding people. Each step seemed to take for ever, though the ground level was thankfully coming up fast.

Before he knew it, he was outside and handing his precious bundle over to her mother. 'There you go, little one.'

'I owe you a beer,' Cameron said as he looked around. 'What a nightmare. I thought it was a practice run, but that smoke's for real.'

'Move along. Everyone needs to congregate on the footpath on the opposite side of the road.' A policewoman was walking through the groups of shocked people. 'Out of the way so the firemen can get access. You all need to register your name and unit number with the two constables over the road. Do not go anywhere until you have.'

A small crowd had already gathered over there. Nick reached into his pocket. No phone. Damn it. He hadn't given it a thought when he'd grabbed his wallet and keys. How was he meant to inform his new boss, Joy, that he'd be late? Great. First day on the job. Not a good impression. According to Joy, he was meant to be going on a flight to Cook Town to pick up a young boy and bring him down here to the hospital for treatment. He needed to move. Fast.

He aimed for the front of the queue of tenants waiting to register their details. 'I'm sorry to push in, but I'm a doctor at Flying Health Care and need to get to work fast.' He might also be needed here of course. 'Unless I can help you out?'

One of the constables looked up. 'Got ID?'

Fair enough. In his wallet, he found his medical licence as well as the pass for the hangar he'd work from and handed them over. 'Here you go.'

'Thanks for the offer of help but the ambos are almost here.'

Nick realised sirens were approaching. 'That's good as I am supposed to be at work shortly. What is the time?' His watch was on his bedside table. When he was told he gasped. Where had the last thirty minutes gone? 'Right, I'll be on my way.'

'Hope your car's not in the apartment block basement.'

His heart sank. No phone. No car. Getting worse by the minute. 'I'll grab a taxi.'

'That ain't happening. The road's closed to all but emergency vehicles.'

Another officer stepped up. 'I'll take you to the airport.'

'Thanks, mate, but surely you're needed here?'

'They can do without me. So far it doesn't appear that anyone's injured, and plenty of other cops are waiting for the all-clear to go inside and check out the apartments to see what happened. It's important to get you where you're needed most. Come on.'

'Cheers, mate.' The guy seemed determined to give Nick a lift. Had someone close to him been saved by the Flying Health Care service?

'It's going to be noisy till we get past the traffic block,' the cop said as he flicked on the siren.

'Nothing I'm not used to on the ambulances.' Nick settled back for the crazy ride. 'You had much to do with Flying Health Care?' Might as well find out more while dealing with the frustration of the traffic jam.

'They flew our daughter to Brisbane Hospital when we were holidaying south of Townsville. She'd drowned and been resuscitated by the life guards but wasn't really responding to them. Scary time, I can tell you. Those guys are heroes.'

'Yes, they are.' Staring out at the backed-up traffic where kids crossed the road to a school, he wondered what lay ahead for him. That sense of finally wanting to stop and put down roots had returned.

Why now? Why here in Cairns? His apartment was like all the others he'd rented over the years since qualifying. A tidy place to cook a meal and put his head down after a long shift at work. He'd met people he enjoyed socialising with in every place he'd lived and worked. There'd been no pressure to get on and make the most of what he had. Yet less than a week in Cairns and the apartment already felt impersonal, despite the furnishings he took everywhere.

The town interested him. There were lots of beaches to enjoy, rural townships to visit, plenty of walking tracks. Nothing unusual except that, for the first time, he was considering staying around for longer than normal.

Leesa had something to do with that. Though he wasn't sure that was such a good idea. After all, this time the images of her smiles, laughter and sexy body were most likely overrated. She'd turn out to be a disappointment if he bumped into her again.

He laughed to himself. Give that time. A few

weeks on the job and he'd probably be changing his mind. Except work was the one thing that always kept him grounded. Along with making him proud. He'd done well training to become an emergency doctor. He still relished every moment on the job as much as he had the very first time he'd stepped into an emergency department as a house surgeon.

'You're new on the block?' the cop asked. 'Haven't seen you around.'

'Moved up last week from Brisbane where I was on the ambulances.'

'You'll find it's not quite as busy up here. Though we do have our share of problems too. Like any town I guess.'

'There are high tourist numbers here and up the coast, aren't there?'

'Yes, but they cause less trouble than the locals. Mostly anyway.'

A road sign indicated the airport was ahead. Nick heaved a sigh of relief. 'That didn't take long.'

'Helps having the right bells and whistles.'

Now to face the day. Hopefully no one would be too disgruntled with him. More than half an hour late wasn't good, but it could've been a lot worse.

'Morning everyone. I'm Dr Nicolas Springer. Joy told me to come on out and get on board. She's tied up with someone from the hospital at the moment.'

You've got to be kidding me.

At the sound of that gravelly voice Leesa's head spun around. She grabbed the door frame of the pilot's cabin to stay upright as she came face to face with their new colleague. Dr Sexy himself.

What were the odds? It had been over a year since he'd left her bed for the final time after lots of the most amazing sex she'd ever known, and still her gut tightened when he spoke. Wonderful. Now what? She had to work alongside that voice. Unless she gagged him every time they shared a shift. 'Hello, Nick.'

His eyes widened. 'Leesa? I knew you'd moved up here and figured we'd probably bump into each other somewhere on the job, but I didn't realise you worked for this lot.'

She could feel her face redden as memories of his hands on her body swamped her. Not appropriate. They were colleagues now. Yeah, so how to stop this reaction? Carry a bottle of cold water all the time?

'Would that have made any difference?' she snapped in an attempt to get back on track. It wasn't as though she'd been hankering for more time with him. No way. Those nights had been so wonderful it was unlikely they could be repeated. Besides, she still didn't do trusting men when it came to her heart. Though she was moving closer to thinking it was time to try again and to hell with the past. And, if she were honest, she had to admit that her passionate fling with Nick had gone a long way to letting her guard down.

'To me accepting the job?' He shook his head. 'Not at all.' He glanced past her and saw the pilot looking back at him, and repeated, 'Hi, I'm Nick.'

'Darren, your pilot today.'

Leesa stepped back as the men shook hands.

The last thing she wanted was to feel Nick's touch. She'd turn into a blob of jelly.

'Look, I'm very sorry to keep you waiting but there was a fire in the apartment block I've moved into, and I wasn't allowed into the basement to get my ute. Fortunately, one of the cops gave me a lift or who knows when I'd have made it.'

'Guess we can't complain about that.' Leesa sighed. It wasn't as if he'd slept in or stopped at the supermarket to get lunch on the way. She was still aghast to learn he was the newest doctor at Flying Health Care. Of all people, he had to be the one she'd prefer not to bump into again. It had taken some time to put it behind her, and already hot images of Nick were reappearing at the front of her mind. Not to mention the tightness in her gut. That was enough to put her off eating for the rest of the day.

She headed through the plane to confirm with

the groundsman they were ready to have the stairway taken away so she could close the door. 'We'd better get a move along. Jacob gets stressed when he has to wait for us to pick him up.' And she needed to focus on work, ignoring Dr Sexy in every other respect.

'Our patient this morning?' Nick asked as he put his backpack away and buckled himself into the spare seat.

'Yes. Once a fortnight we transport him from Cook Town down here for treatment. He has acute lymphatic leukaemia and has just started his second month of chemotherapy. He stays overnight, sometimes two nights depending how he does, which lately has been tough on him. When he's cleared to go home, we give him a lift back. The road trip is too far for the little guy.'

'How old is he?'

'Eight. He's the cheekiest kid about and we all adore him. Even when he's stressed.' She hated when Jacob got upset. She might be a paramedic and see a lot of distress on the job, but it still hurt to witness anyone, particularly a child, in pain or ill or frightened about what they were going through. How parents coped was beyond her. These scenarios had to be their absolute worst nightmare.

Darren came through the headset. 'All tied in back there?'

'Ready and waiting.' Leesa sank into her seat and stared out at the tarmac beyond. In the distance a passenger plane was beginning take off. It was a superb day with the sun shining and no wind. That wouldn't last. The sea breeze would make itself known later in the day.

Dr Nicolas Springer. Nick, in other words. Dr Sexy. No, she wasn't going there. That was behind them. Anyway, he was good looking and appeared to be a great guy—he probably wasn't on his own any more. Not that she one hundred percent knew if he'd had anyone special in his life back when they got together, but for some reason she'd trusted him. Which was plain dumb, considering how she'd trusted her ex not to be a bully and got that so wrong. Her trust was no longer given so easily under normal circumstances, and her affair with Nick had certainly been a moment out of time. One she hadn't regretted at all.

The propellers began spinning, rapidly gaining speed. Leesa watched as they rolled towards the tarmac, absorbing the thrill this always gave her. Sometimes she thought about getting her private pilot's licence for small planes, but then where would she fly to? Cairns was a long way from anywhere except the many small outlying communities. It was better to let the professionals give her a buzz.

'Is this the job you came to after leaving Brisbane?' Nick asked.

'Yes. It's the best one I've ever had. I especially get a kick out of helping kids and their families.'

'That's one reason I applied to work here. Helping people who want us there for them during difficult times. I've had enough of the abuse we get on the ambulances. Drunks thinking they should get special treatment, or fighting what you're trying to do to help them.' He shook his head. 'Sometimes it makes me wonder why we go to so much trouble to aid people, and then the next patient is wonderful and I have my answer.'

Blimey, he could be talkative. Not how she remembered him. The circumstances couldn't be more different though. They were at work, not having a drink or dancing. Or—yes, well, enough.

'I get what you're saying, and on these flights we mostly get gratitude.' There was the odd exception when someone thought they should be treated like royalty because they'd paid for their flight. Not all trips were provided by the health system. As far as she was concerned, everyone got the best help possible, irrelevant of who was paying and how old the patient was.

'Makes sense.' Nick settled back and studied the interior of the plane. 'I need to familiarise myself with everything. I like to be more than one hundred percent on board with it all. I don't want to waste time looking for equipment in an emergency.'

No one wanted that, and he was only doing what everyone did when they first started flying with this outfit. 'Go for it.'

Her pulse was still racing. All she'd known before he stepped on board minutes ago was that the new doctor was named Nicolas Springer and had been working on ambulances all over the country. Not once, even for a moment, had she thought Nicolas might be the Nick she'd spent those fiery nights with. 'What do you prefer to be called? Nick or Nicolas?'

'No one's ever asked me that before.' His focus was now on her. 'Nick. Nicolas is more formal.'

'What do your family call you?'

His mouth tightened. 'Either, or.' His focus returned to the emergency equipment.

Seemed she'd touched a raw nerve. Which was kind of sad if family was an issue for him. Everyone deserved a great family. In reality that wasn't always the case, but she'd been lucky with hers and still believed most people were, despite what she'd seen over the years, first as a nurse then a paramedic. 'I didn't recognise your name when Joy told us you were joining the gang. But we didn't exactly talk much about ourselves, did we?'

Jeez, Leesa, shut up, will you? Her head needed a slap.

'Sorry, forget I said that.'

'We can't avoid the fact we've spent time together, but it is in the past.'

Sometimes honesty could be a bit too blunt. He either wasn't wasting time remembering their time together or was letting her know how little it had meant, just as she should him.

'Yep, it definitely is,' she muttered and opened Jacob's case notes even though she pretty much knew them off by heart.

'I don't want to go to hospital.' Jacob stood near the steps up to the plane with his arms folded and tears pouring down his face. He stamped his foot and shouted, 'I'm not going.'

Leesa knelt down in front of her favourite little patient, resisting the urge to hug him tight. That wouldn't achieve anything until she knew what the problem was. 'Hey, Jacob, what's up, man? You love flying in the plane.'

'I don't want to.'

'Why not? What's happened to change your mind?'

'I don't like being sick. It's not fair.'

Leesa couldn't agree more. Glancing over to his mother, she noted the worry emanating from Kerry's tired eyes and gave her a smile that hopefully said, 'I've got this,' when she had no idea what was going on.

Even when he was stressed about what lay ahead in Cairns, Jacob was usually compliant when he had to board his ride. She sat down on the ground and reached out a hand. 'Sit with me.' She held her breath as the boy stared at her before slowly sinking down beside her. 'Isn't it cool being allowed on the airport tarmac?'

'It's my friend's birthday today and I want to go to his house and give him my present.'

Now she got it. Her heart broke for Jacob. Being so ill was hard for anyone, but for a child who didn't fully understand everything only made it twice as difficult. Though sometimes she suspected there wasn't much this boy didn't get about his condition. Today's reaction would be fairly normal even for adults.

'I bet you do, but you know what? He'll get lots of presents today so when you come home later in the week and give him yours it will be the only one that day, and that'll make it special.'

Jacob stared at her. 'I want to give it to him today. Everyone else is.' He wanted to be normal like his pals.

'I've got an idea. You could ring him later when you know he's home from school and sing *Happy Birthday*. That'd be special, wouldn't it?'

'Yeah.' A little bit of tension left Jacob's face. 'I s'pose.'

'You can practice singing the song all the way to Cairns.' Hopefully they had a quick flight.

'Will you sing with me?'

A gravelly laugh came from behind them. 'Go, kid.'

She grinned but didn't look over her shoulder at Nick, even though she wanted to see that sexy face with the neatly trimmed beard. What if she started calling him Nicolas? Would that be less sexy? Except it wasn't his name that set her blood racing.

'You'll regret asking me. I sound like a dog under water when I sing.'

'Max's having a party on the weekend. I have to stop being sick by then.'

'Then the sooner we get you to hospital the sooner you will have your treatment and start getting over it.' Of course she was exaggerating, but if it worked then what the heck? This kid had to have his chemo. Along with as normal a life as possible.

Jacob stood up and held out his hand to her. 'Come on then.'

'Cool.' Relief filled her.

'Thank you so much, Leesa,' Kerry said. 'He's been upset all morning and I just didn't know what to do.'

'You were brilliant,' Nick said quietly, sounding a little awe struck.

She'd take that as a compliment, especially from this man. 'Jacob knows the drill and will be fine now.'

And he was, talking excitedly to the new doctor, telling him how the plane worked and where they were going to land and how the pilot had to look out for other planes flying in the sky.

Leesa relaxed, glad that Jacob had moved on from his distress. It was hard enough going through the treatment without being upset over missing out on fun with his friends.

When they disembarked at Cairns he was still yabbering to Nick, pulling him along by the hand and telling him not to be so slow because he had to get his treatment done so he could ring his friend.

'Quite the little charmer, isn't he?' Nick said when the ambulance had left with Jacob and Kerry.

'It breaks my heart to see what he's going through.'

'You're amazing. The way you took your time to persuade him to get on board made all the difference.'

'How else would I deal with it? He's got enough going on without needing a bossy paramedic telling him to do what he's told.'

Nick touched her arm. 'I agree with you whole-heartedly. But it was special, Leesa. I've never seen anyone deal with a distraught young patient quite like that.'

Someone else who was a charmer, huh? She knew all about them. Shrugging, she said, 'Let's grab a coffee while it's quiet.' There was a warmth where his hand had touched her that had nothing to do with the balmy warm winter temperature. It was a familiar sensation from the past. Except then there'd been nothing warm about what went on between them. No, it had been all hot. Searing hot. Something she wasn't meant to remember at all.

'Do we know what our next job is?' Obviously, Nick wasn't affected by her in any way.

'We're taking a teenage girl home to Mackay once she's been discharged from Paediatric Orthopaedics. She was in a serious quad bike accident two and a half weeks ago and has multiple fractures to both legs. Her mother is a solo mum and a GP. She's going to look after her daughter around her job as it's easier than coming back and forth to Cairns every night after work to be with her.'

'Who's going to be with the girl while her mother's at work?'

'I've been told she practises from rooms at home, and she employs a nurse as well who'll also keep an eye on Matilda. It's going to be a difficult couple of months for them.'

'You certainly see a painful side of parenting in this job, don't you?'

'True, we do, but we also see wonderful parents coping with their worst nightmares while supporting and encouraging their children through hell.'

Another touch on her arm. 'You're very empathetic. I like that too.'

Too? What else about her was ticking his boxes? Did she even want that to be happening? As much as she'd liked him, she really wasn't ready to get to know him any better. Apparently, he moved around a lot and that wasn't her style. She preferred to be grounded in one place where she had family and friends.

She'd gone to Brisbane because her then husband had wanted to take up a great career opportunity, and in her book supporting him was part of being together. She should've read Connor's book first, then she'd never have married him, let alone left Cairns.

'You talk more than I remember.' Here she went again, raising the one subject that was taboo because she didn't need to go there. Make that she didn't want to, as it brought back wonderful memories that were unlikely to ever be repeated.

'We were usually too busy to talk.'

She had no idea how to respond to that statement. He definitely had no qualms about mentioning their time together. He'd have to learn that she did, except she wasn't actually doing any better thinking about it.

They reached the hangar where Darren was standing in the kitchen doorway with a full coffee plunger. The tightness in her gut eased a tad.

'You drink coffee or tea?' Darren nodded at the man striding alongside her.

'Coffee's good.'

Joy appeared behind Darren and the conversation turned to work and all things acceptable in Leesa's thinking.

Not that she could drop the mental picture of that long, muscular body wrapped around hers after they'd made love. Nick had been extraordinary, and lifted the bar for her. Which could make things tricky going forward. She'd always be looking out for another Dr Sexy. Had been since she'd moved back here, though cautiously, in case she found another bad one.

'So, you two know each other?' Joy cut through her thoughts.

'Umm, briefly,' Leesa replied uneasily.

'Not really,' Nick said at the same time.

Joy gave them both a studied look. 'As long as nothing gets in the way of you working together then we'll leave the subject alone.'

It seemed Joy suspected there was more to the story than either of them were letting on. So what? It had nothing to do with work, hadn't even happened in Cairns, so there wouldn't be a problem. Apart from the rattled sensation she got when too close to Dr Sexy.

Leesa turned away to stir sugar into her coffee, ignoring the raised eyebrows of her colleagues. Nosey lot. She was hardly going to announce to everyone that she'd had a one-night stand with the new doctor—which had turned into a five-night stand. Dropping the teaspoon in the sink, she got her lunch out of the fridge and took a seat at the tiny table where everyone knocked elbows all the time.

Nick was leaning against the bench, coffee in hand.

Of course. 'You didn't have a chance to get any lunch, did you?'

'I'm good.'

In other words, no. 'There're yoghurts in the fridge and I've got a couple of bananas in my locker.'

'Girl food,' Darren retorted. 'Here, man, have one of my sandwiches. My wife always makes too many.'

'Cheers, Darren. If you're sure?' Nick reached for a sandwich, not looking her way once.

Awkward.

* * *

'Matilda, can you hear me?' Nick asked the teenager lying on the trolley bed.

Apart from the dark shadows beneath her eyes, her face was very pale. 'Yes, Doctor.'

'Good. We're going to get you inside the plane now. We'll be careful not to jar you in any way, but if you feel pain please tell us.'

Matilda did the defiant teen eye-roll thing. 'You think?'

'More pain than you're already feeling.' He knew from the notes she was on strong medication, but it wouldn't take much to inflict more hurt. 'Let's do this, Leesa.'

Leesa, the woman who'd toyed with his mind ever since their short fling in her apartment, which had then become his apartment. Until he'd packed up to come north, only to bump into Leesa so soon. It seemed as if something out there was toying with them, bringing them together at every opportunity. Were they meant to be together?

Try again. Nick shivered as he lifted his end of the trolley. They were stepping around each other, as if afraid to relax in each other's company, when not with a patient to deflect any thoughts they might have about their brief past. It could get tricky when they had to spend quite a bit of time together.

He usually dated women who loved having a bit of fun and then moved on. While getting involved with someone who wanted the whole shooting box was his dream, it was also scary beyond description. He had no idea if Leesa wanted the same. She appeared comfortable with her lifestyle, whatever that was, but that didn't make risking his heart again any easier.

His ex Ellie's revelation about the pregnancy, and that there'd been other men in her bed after they'd married, had taught him not to believe anyone when they said they loved him. Of course, he wanted nothing more than a woman to love for ever and who'd love him equally.

The only person he remembered ever loving him unconditionally was his grandfather, who'd passed away when he was twelve. He didn't remember anything about his parents, as they'd been killed in a car crash when he was barely a year old. Now here he was in Cairns working alongside Leesa, who'd got to him in lots of ways. Was that why he'd moved north? He wasn't sure, but suspected she'd had at least some part to play in it.

'How's that, Matilda?' Leesa asked their patient, more focused on the job than he apparently was. He'd say she was deliberately avoiding him as much as was professionally possible.

If Leesa was going to be such a distraction,

then he'd have to ask Joy to roster him with other staff and never her. Might as well hand in his notice and move on now then, because that would be impossible with the small number of medics working the shifts. 'How's the pain level, Matilda?'

'You did a good job,' the teen retorted. 'No change.'

'Glad I'm good for something,' he grinned, comfortable with the patient if not his work partner. 'Let's get you tied down so we can get out of here.'

'You're making me sound like a wild pig you've just caught.' She giggled.

At last. Nick sighed, pleased to have lifted his patient's spirits, if only a little. He wasn't quite as good as Leesa with difficult patients, but he'd managed to make this one smile. 'One way of looking at it.'

Leesa was attaching monitors. 'Just keeping tabs on your blood pressure during the flight, Matilda.'

'Is that necessary?'

'I like to be cautious.' Leesa smiled. 'It's all part of the package.' Her gaze swept over him, wariness blinking out of those beautiful green eyes.

She hadn't been cautious the night they first met. Heat filled him. Just like that. Too easy.

Yep, he definitely should ask to work with someone else. Except Leesa had been so good with Jacob he wanted to work alongside her. He'd had to blink fast as she talked the boy into calming down and doing what was required. Leesa was special. But then he'd already suspected that. Which still wasn't a reason to spend more time than required on duty with her. Even then, he needed to keep her at arm's length. Like that was going to be possible inside a small plane.

Leesa shut the door and leaned into the cockpit. 'We're good to go, Darren.'

'We've got a five-minute wait. A flight from Sydney's on finals.'

'No prob.' Buckling herself in, she glanced his way. 'What do you think so far?'

About her? Amazing. *Yeah, right. Get a grip.* 'Flying in a plane certainly beats sitting in an ambulance, being held up in traffic mayhem at peak times.'

'Thankfully it doesn't get that busy in the sky.' She looked at the teenager and a frown appeared. 'Matilda, do you like flying?'

The girl was clenching and unclenching her hands. 'I've only been in a chopper and that wasn't nice.'

Nick asked, 'Was that the day of your accident?'

'Yeah.' Her hands tightened.

'You'll find riding in a plane a lot smoother than in a helicopter.' In an attempt to distract her, he asked, 'What happened? I heard you were in a quad bike accident.'

'I hit the accelerator instead of the brake and went over a bank. The bike landed on top of me.'

No wonder her memories of flying in a helicopter weren't wonderful. She'd have been in horrendous pain and shock, along with probably being frightened about what was going to happen to her. The case notes were on the end of the trolley. He picked them up. 'That must've been scary.'

'Try terrifying.'

Leesa stretched across to hold Matilda's nearest hand. 'Today will be a lot better. Darren's a great pilot, there's no wind to make it a bumpy ride, and you're in a lot better place than you were that day.'

'Were you with me?' Matilda asked her.

'I was. You gave that quad bike quite a fight.'

The signature eye roll appeared. 'I wish that were true.'

The notes Nick scanned made hideous reading. Three fractures in the left leg and two in the right. Five broken ribs added to the count. 'You're very lucky not to have sustained more serious injuries.' How Matilda avoided internal damage was beyond him.

'Thanks a lot, Doc. I don't see the luck in that, but if you say so I'll go along with it.'

Outside the windows the props began turning. Matilda's eyes widened and she gripped Leesa so hard it was a wonder bones weren't breaking in Leesa's hand. 'I remember this. It's like the chopper, how the noise gets louder and louder. I thought I was going to be in another accident.'

'Surely you were on strong painkillers?' Nick said.

'They didn't stop me thinking awful things.'

'They probably added to your mental confusion,' he told her. 'Today you can relax and take in what happens as we leave the ground and fly to your home town. You might even like the experience this time. How's that pulse?' he asked Leesa as she finished checking it with her free hand.

'As normal as any fifteen-year-old on an out-of-this-world experience can be.' She smiled at Matilda before turning and giving him one too. 'Up a little,' she mouthed.

Not surprised given Matilda's stress, he nodded. 'Wonder if we'll see any UFOs today.'

Another eye roll. 'You're nuts, Doc.'

'I've been called worse.' The silly talk was working though, as she didn't seem to realise they were already lined up at the end of the runway.

'Argh.' Matilda's cry of pain had him unclipping his belt and jumping out of his seat.

'What's up?'

'I moved my leg. Or I tried. It usually moves with a bit of effort.'

'Which leg?'

'The right one.'

The cast held it straight, so movement shouldn't have affected the fractures. 'Where exactly did you feel pain?'

Leesa was checking the BP monitor. 'All good.'

'Top of my thigh.'

The femur was fractured near the knee, not by the hip. 'Have you felt pain here before?' His fingers worked over the muscles.

Matilda winced. 'Sometimes when I've tried to roll over in my sleep.'

'I'd say it's happening in your muscles. Currently they're not being used, your movement went against what the casts are trying to prevent so they reacted.' He pressed lightly. 'How does it feel here?'

'All right. They told me the same in hospital but sometimes I forget.'

'You might need to have some massages,' Leesa said. 'Or get your mum to do it. I presume doctors have a basic idea?' she asked him.

'Very basic, but that's all Matilda needs.'

Matilda closed her eyes, like she had had enough of the conversation. She didn't appear to have noticed they were airborne and climbing rapidly, or wasn't concerned this time after all.

Nick returned to his seat. 'Where are we landing? I presume there's an airstrip near the town.'

'There's one right on the outskirts, about half a kilometre from Matilda's home. The local ambulance crew will transport her from there to the house.'

'Then we'll be on our way again.' Different to being in the ambulance, not knowing where or when the next call out will come. 'Do we know what's next?'

'Coffee?'

That cheeky glint in her eyes wound him up tight all over again. He knew what he'd like instead of coffee, and it didn't come in a mug. More of a rerun of some certain nights. 'Sounds like a plan.'

'Followed by taking a fifty-one-year-old woman to Townsville. She has early onset dementia, she's been in Cairns for respite care while her husband arranges permanent accommodation for her in the local rest home.'

Flying Health Care catered for all sorts of illnesses and emergencies. It was all about making the most of the staff and aircraft. They also covered emergencies with the Fire and Emergency Service with a helicopter when necessary. 'Every call is different, isn't it?'

'Makes the job exciting.'

At the moment Leesa was doing that. Not a good look for a doctor who needed to be fully focused on the case in hand. The doctor he'd always been until this morning. His phone pinged. Grateful for the interruption he looked at the message and glanced across to Leesa. 'The cop who drove me to the airport says the apartment building's been given the all-clear and everyone's allowed back in.'

'Did he say what caused the smoke? Or fire?'

'Someone on the floor below mine left a pot on the gas ring with oil in it and went out for a run.' *Idiot.* 'I'm glad the smoke detectors came on fast or who knows what the outcome might have been.'

'So you're renting another apartment.'

'Yes.' No ties that way. When he decided to move on, he only had to pack his bags and call in the furniture moving company.

Leesa stared at him for a moment. 'Why not a house?'

His shrug was deliberate. 'Suits me best.'

'Right.' Disappointment blinked out of those thoughtful eyes before she turned away.

What did she expect? A full explanation about how, after his grandfather passed away, he'd grown up in foster homes, where no one cared about giving him a loving environment to enjoy and get used to? It was the driving force behind why he never stayed in one place for too long. The max was a couple of years, not always that long.

But that wasn't something he put out there. He didn't want anyone feeling sorry for him. He'd done enough of that all by himself in years gone by. Now he got on with making life work for him without getting too involved with anyone, though he stayed in regular contact with Logan.

'How're you doing, Matilda? That leg settling down?'

'Kind of.'

'I can't give you any more painkillers. You've had maximum dosage.'

'Whatever.' Typical teen response.

He leaned back and stared out the tiny window at the passing sky. The sense that the time had come to turn his life around had begun on the night he'd met Leesa at that barbecue, the ensuing nights only intensifying the idea.

She'd been the opposite of the women he usually knew, but there'd also been something about her quiet demeanour that had drawn him to her. She hadn't been quiet all the time, but for the first hour, as they'd sat having a drink and watching everyone else enjoying themselves, she had. He'd told himself to get up and leave, because there was a confident yet wary air about her. It had him wondering if he should try for a future that held the promise of the love he craved. But it had proved impossible to walk away. Look at the fun he'd had because of that—and the memories that haunted him.

Over the intervening months he hadn't stopped thinking about her, and what could be out there for him if only he could let go of the fierce need to protect himself. All because of a few nights spent with Leesa.

So was she the reason he'd come to Cairns? Along with the wake-up call after Patrick's cancer scare? Really? It couldn't be. That was too much to believe. Wasn't it?

He'd taken over her Brisbane apartment as a way of keeping her near in a vague kind of way. Though he'd quickly learned Leesa wasn't exactly unknown in the Brisbane emergency services, after all she'd done to help the women being abused by the previous boss of the ambulance station. Most people were in awe of her, but naturally there were a few who thought she should've minded her own business. Personally, he thought she had to have been very gutsy to do what she did, never mind the outcome for herself.

Had he truly moved north to get to know her better? Deeper? His mouth dried as he realised it was very likely why he'd gone online looking for a position up here, instead of reading all the situations vacant in the ambulance field over the whole country as per usual. Though not for one moment had he expected to be working out of the same base as her. He'd thought she'd be on the ambulances, not in the air. 'Idiot.'

'Pardon?' Leesa asked.

'Nothing. Ignore me.' For ever.

CHAPTER TWO

LEESA TOSSED HER car key in the air and caught it again. Offering Nick a ride home since he didn't have his vehicle would be the right thing to do. But then she'd have to cope with him sitting in the car beside her, taking up all the air and space, while setting a new rhythm to her heartbeat.

There were plenty of taxis over at the terminal building. He'd be fine. And she'd be selfish to drive off without offering him a lift. It wasn't an invitation to get close again.

Remember that the next time you get all hot around him.

'Nick,' she called, looking around for that tall, well-honed body that had taken over the interior of the plane like he owned it.

'What's up?' He came up behind her.

Her palms tingled. 'Do you want a lift to your apartment?'

'That'd be great, thanks.'

No hesitation about accepting her offer. More proof she wasn't upsetting him the way he did her. 'Let's go then.' She wanted this over and done, then she could pick up Baxter, head back to the house Gran had lent her and give the dog a walk before relaxing over a cold beer after an unusual day.

The cases had been much the same as usual, except there'd been no emergencies or a patient going bad on them. It was Dr Sexy who'd really upset her equilibrium. Something she needed to get over fast because they would work together a lot. Not every shift was with the same person, but more than enough to worry her. He still had the power to turn her on fast. More than a year had gone by since they'd been so intimate, and yet the moment she'd heard his voice when he boarded the plane she'd been in trouble.

'I'll just grab my bag.'

'I'll be out in the carpark.' She wasn't hanging around inside waiting for him. That'd seem too eager, wouldn't it? Or normal for some people. Not for her. At the moment not a lot felt normal, all because Nick had turned up in her life again, and this time for more than a few nights.

Twenty minutes later Nick strolled out to join her. 'Sorry, Joy cornered me. She wanted to know how the day had gone and had I enjoyed the work.'

'Did you?' Did Joy mention again the fact Nick knew her?

'Absolutely. It's different to what I've done before in that we seem to get closer to the patients and learn more about them because there are repeat visits. If Jacob hadn't already spent time in your care, it might've been harder to calm him down and get him on board without a bigger fuss.' Then he shook his head. 'I take that back. You'd have managed no matter what. You have a way about you that has patients eating out of your hand.'

Nothing awkward about that. Opening her door, she looked at him over the car roof. He really thought that? Yes, he would, because from the little she knew he wasn't a man to say something he didn't believe. *Wow.*

'Let's hope whatever it is, it keeps working,' Leesa replied. 'There're times when patients seriously need to calm down for their own safety, and if they didn't listen to us, we'd have a load of problems on our hands.'

She got into the car before she said too much. Just looking at Nick undid a lot of the determination to keep her distance. Pulling on her straight-face look, she turned on the ignition and music filled the car. One of the songs they'd danced to in the park by her old apartment, to be exact. Heat tore up her face. That was happening a lot today. She flicked the sound off.

'You don't have to turn it off for my sake.'

But she had to for hers. She'd downloaded the music and sung her heart out on the long drive home from Brisbane. She'd tried telling herself it was because she loved the tunes, that it had nothing to do with how she'd felt exhilarated and happy dancing and making out with Nick. 'I have it too loud sometimes.'

'It's the only way to listen to good music.' He grinned.

That damned grin was too sexy for her to be able to switch off the emotions it brought on. Putting the car in drive, she didn't waste any time heading out of the airport perimeter. The sooner her passenger was out of the car the better. She'd be able to breathe freely, for one.

'The apartment block's on George Street.'

'Right.' She hadn't thought to ask where they were headed. Another mistake, all because Nick was so distracting it was becoming embarrassing.

'Know where that is?'

'Yes.' She could do uncommunicative. Safer than saying something she'd instantly regret, which she seemed to do an awful lot around Nick.

He must've got the message because he said no more until she turned into his street and parked outside the apartment building. Looking around, he said, 'Not a sign of what went on this morning.'

'Why would there be?'

He shrugged. 'Don't know really. Want a beer?'

Love one.

'No, thanks. I've got to take my dog for a walk.'

'Okay.' He shoved the door open. 'Where do you go walking?'

'I'll take him along the promenade.' It wasn't far from here and Baxter would be chomping at the bit to get out and about. So much for going home first. Something else to put on Nick?

'Mind if I come with you?'

What? Nick wanted to join her for a walk? Outside of work? After she'd made an idiot of herself with that music.

He was watching her too closely. 'I think we need to clear the air if we're going to get along at work.'

'We got along fine today.' She'd liked working with him. He took his job very seriously. They all did. It was her dream job, and not once had she regretted returning home. But now Nick had landed on her workplace doorstep that might change everything.

Only if I let him.

True. She was in charge of her own destiny, something she'd repeatedly told herself over the years dealing with bullies. While Nick wasn't a bully—as far as she'd seen anyway, but she'd got that wrong in the past so would always be wary—he did seem to hold sway over her emotions. That needed dealing with sooner than later. He was already changing her, in that she did want to get to know him better and to have some fun. Like between the sheets again? It had been incredible before.

He was still watching her.

She sighed. 'You're right. Close the door and we'll go pick up Baxter.'

'I'm not trying to cause trouble, Leesa. I know I've landed on your patch and I don't want you to regret my arrival. We're adults. We can work together without that brief fling causing trouble between us.'

Blunt for sure. Also correct. 'Of course we can.' She went for honesty. 'I enjoyed today. You're a great doctor, and good with our patients. They liked you.'

I was relaxed when I wasn't recalling how your hands felt on my body, which was most of the time.

Feeling her face redden, she indicated to pull out and drove away from the apartment block.

Nick said nothing more until she pulled up outside a building with a high fenced yard, where a few dogs were waiting impatiently for their owners to turn up. 'You put your dog in day care?' He grinned. 'You are such a softie.'

'So what?'

'Just saying. I'm not surprised after seeing how you handled Jacob.'

Relax, Leesa. Give the guy a break.

'Baxter came from a rescue centre. His previous owners used to leave him tied up for days on end with little food or water, so I just can't tie him up and go out for very long. He gets distressed believing I'm going to leave him there for days, so when I've got something to go to other than work, I leave him with Mum and Dad.'

'How can people be so cruel?' Nick shook his head. 'Why have a dog if you're going to treat it like that?'

'The million-dollar question. Won't be a moment.' Out of the car, she strode inside to collect her beloved four-legged boy who was wagging his tail frantically as always. She knew he never expected her to come and pick him up, but at least here he was petted and loved by the staff running the centre while he waited for her to reappear.

'Hey, there, Leesa. Baxter's chomping at the bit to go home,' Karin said as she clipped the dog lead on. 'There you go, fella. Mum's here.'

Leesa dropped to her knees to hug her pet. 'Hello, Gorgeous. Had a good day?'

Baxter pushed into her, his lean body hard up against her.

'That's a yes then. We're off to walk the esplanade.' Standing up, she took the lead. 'See you tomorrow, Karin.'

Outside Baxter bounced up and down to the car, then stopped and stared at Nick through the window.

'It's all right, boy. Nick's a friend.' Sort of.

Nick opened his door and got out, holding his hands out for Baxter to sniff. 'Hey, Baxter.' He kept his voice light and calm.

Baxter sat back and looked up at him.

'Give him a moment,' she said. 'He's cautious around new people.'

'Wise dog.'

'There you go.' Her boy had stood up and was sniffing Nick's hand. 'You're in.' Easy as. But then she'd been much the same when she first met Nick. Would be again if she didn't keep a watch over herself. Sudden laughter bubbled up. She really was mad, and right now she didn't care at all.

'What's funny?' Nick looked as though he'd like something to laugh about too.

Good question. She wasn't really sure. 'Dogs. Men.'

He stared at her, then finally laughed too. 'Add women and we're on the same page.'

'Fair enough.' Opening the back door, she indicated for Baxter to get in so she could put on his safety harness. 'Let's go.'

* * *

Why had he suggested he join Leesa for the walk? Nick wondered as they strolled along the esplanade with Baxter bounding ahead. It was all very well saying they needed to iron out the hitches between them, but he had no idea where to start. Seemed Leesa didn't either, as she was staying very quiet except for an occasional word to the dog. She was probably waiting to see where he was going with this—it was his suggestion in the first place.

'Unreal.'

'What is?' she asked without looking his way.

He could say the stunning outlook across the harbour, but that'd be avoiding her. 'That I started work today at the same place you're employed. What were the odds?'

'Fairly high, I'd have thought. Cairns isn't a huge city and there aren't numerous air or road ambulance services.' Sarcasm dripped off her tongue. 'Did it never occur to you that you might end up at the same place?' It was coming across in spades that she wasn't pleased.

'I wondered if our paths might cross, but I didn't expect to end up at the same service centre.' He had thought about what it would be like to work for the same company, and hadn't really come up with a satisfactory answer. It was feeling more and more like he really had wanted to meet up again. Going by her reactions over the day, Leesa probably hadn't given much thought to their fling, other than maybe she didn't want anything more to do with him. She was blunt at times and friendly at others, but never fully relaxed.

'Face it, I know very little about you, and for all I know you might be like me and move around a lot.' He winced. He'd said too much about himself.

'I'm the dead opposite. I grew up here and the only other place I've lived is Brisbane.'

'I've no idea what it's like to live in one area for most of your life.' He could add that made him feel a little bit jealous, but best he didn't. She'd want an explanation he wasn't prepared to give.

Prepared? Or ready? As in he might eventually want to take the risk of exposing his inner demons? He'd already said too much. Coming on this walk with Leesa hadn't been his brightest idea. She had the ability to make him want to talk about things he never discussed with anyone.

'I'm sorry to hear that.' The tension had gone from her shoulders. There was a quizzical look in her eyes when she glanced across at him.

Don't ask why.

'Baxter's happy.'

'Nick, relax. I'm not going to pummel you with questions. Since we met in Brisbane, I have sometimes wondered what you were up to and if you were happy there. You're an okay guy and I'm happy to be working with you.' There was some heat creeping into her face and she'd begun walking faster. 'I don't see any reason for Joy to worry about us.'

'I agree.' He upped his pace to keep beside her. 'Thank you for making it easy. It can be tricky spending a lot of time with someone after what we enjoyed that week.' At least he hoped she'd enjoyed it. By the ecstatic sounds that came from her mouth at certain moments he was certain she had. He didn't believe she'd faked any of their love making. Sex, man. It was sex, pure and simple. Except never before had he spent so much time thinking about a woman he'd had sex with. Nothing pure and simple about that.

'My job is the most important thing I do and I won't let anything jeopardise it. Not even get offside with you,' she added with a tight smile.

'Good. Shall we start afresh by having a meal at one of the cafes on the other side of the road?'

'Meal? Flip. Sorry, I have to phone Mum. I'm meant to be having dinner with her and Dad.' She tugged her phone from her back pocket and tapped the screen. 'Mum? I'm going to be late. Sorry, but I was caught up in work stuff.' She glanced at him and grimaced. 'Now I'm walking Baxter and the doctor who started on the job today. He was at a loose end.'

'You're walking me?' He laughed.

She started to smile. 'Get in behind.' Then her smile vanished. 'Really? Maybe not.' Her sigh was dramatic. 'Okay, I'll ask him but we'll be late.' She held her phone away from her ear. 'Mum wants to know if you'd like to join us for dinner.'

Obviously, Leesa wasn't too happy with that idea. He wouldn't mind spending more time with her, but not if she wasn't keen for him to join the family.

'Nick?'

He thought she didn't want him joining her. But it would mean he'd be getting to know Leesa better. No, not yet. If ever. 'Thank you but not tonight. I've some chores to do.'

'Did you hear that, Mum? Nick's got other things on.' He couldn't make out if she was happy or not. 'I'll head back to the car now and be on my way ASAP.' The phone slid back into her pocket. 'Come on, Baxter, we're going to Ma and Pa's for dinner.'

'Leesa.' He paused, uncertain what to say without making matters worse.

'It's fine, Nick. Probably for the best.'

Silence hung between them as they walked back to the car and set off for his apartment.

Finally unable to stand it any longer, he asked, 'Where do your parents live?'

'Twenty-five minutes north of the city. Dad grows sugarcane, has done for decades. He thought my brother might want to continue with the farm but Kevin took up commercial fishing. He works out of Port Douglas, about an hour from here.' It was as though she'd grabbed the chance to talk without going over what hung between them.

'Sounds like a busy family.'

'It was drilled into us as kids that you've got to work for what you want. Nothing comes in a Christmas cracker apparently, though I did keep pulling them in the hope Dad was wrong.'

Silence fell between them, making him wish he'd said yes to dinner with her family, but deep down he wasn't ready for that. Maybe when they were fully established as colleagues and not ex-lovers it would work. Or when he had the guts to follow up on the feelings of need and wonder for Leesa he was desperately trying to deny.

Leaning forward he turned the music up to fill the silence. The blasted song they'd danced to that night.

Leesa threw him a quick glance. 'You stirring, by any chance?'

'Not at all. I like that tune. Also, we agreed we needed to lay the past to rest, so turning music off because we heard it that first night isn't going to help.' Not saying he liked the memories it invoked—hot memories of Leesa dancing, kissing, sharing her body. Should never have turned the damned sound up.

'Of course.'

'Leesa, I'm not saying I want to forget the time we had together.' No way in hell could he. He'd tried and tried, and still the memories taunted him. 'Only now we work together things are different.' Get it? There wouldn't be any more time between the sheets for them.

'Right.'

He had no idea what she thought. Fortunately, his street appeared and Leesa turned the corner a little fast. Eager to get rid of him?

When she pulled up, she surprised him. 'Nick.' Her hand was warm on his bare arm. And electric. Like she'd flicked a switch so a powerful current raced through him. 'Your honesty is confronting but I'm grateful. I don't like ducking and diving around a problem, and yet I confess I've been doing exactly that all day.'

It was quite exciting realising he didn't, and wouldn't, always know what would come out of that sexy mouth. He gave her a smile. 'See you tomorrow.'

CHAPTER THREE

ON FRIDAY MORNING Leesa arrived at the hangar early, determined to find out who she was rostered with and sort her day out before Nick arrived. That way she'd feel in control of something at least.

'Morning, Leesa.'

So much for that idea. 'Hi there.'

Who are you working with?

Even on the days they hadn't worked together during the week she'd been aware of him whenever they were at the base at the same time, which had been often. The roster was lighter than usual.

'I'm on with you today.' So, he did mind reading too. Or just got on with the day. That was more likely as he was a practical man. Among other things.

'Have you checked the list for what's up first?'

Be tough, don't give in to the beating going on in your chest. Practise so that if you do apply for and get Joy's job, you'll know how to cope with left-field problems.

Like Nick, except she'd have to keep well away from anything more than a working relationship with him if she got the job. Since Joy had told her yesterday that she was leaving in eight weeks she'd been tossing the idea around about applying for the position.

A part of her wanted to advance her career, but a deeper part understood it was working with people needing medical help that really ticked her boxes, not sitting in an office doing paperwork for hours. There was nothing to lose thinking about what the job involved. She could always withdraw her application if she decided it wasn't for her. Plus, she'd have something other than Nick to think about.

'Should be a straightforward trip.'

'What?' She'd missed everything he said.

He stared at her and enunciated his words clearly. 'We're picking up a fourteen-year-old boy from Cook Town. He's got an infected club foot.'

'Not something they can deal with at the local hospital?' She really wasn't concentrating. The doctors up in Cook Town wouldn't send the boy their way unless there was a problem.

'Apparently it's serious, the lad didn't go to the doctor until he could barely stand on it.'

'Wonderful,' she muttered. Why did people wait until their condition was so far gone before getting help? It only caused more problems.

'You'd think he'd have learned what to do by his age.'

'Could be he gets teased about his foot and doesn't want to make a fuss.'

Air huffed over her bottom lip. 'I should've thought of that. I know all too well how kids love to tease or bully anyone who doesn't fit in.'

'I heard about what you did for those two women at the ambulance base in Brisbane. Pretty impressive. Not many people stand up to bullies the way you did.'

'I have experience of being bullied.'

His eyes widened. 'Why? You're beautiful and kind and not disdainful of anyone that I've seen.'

Her heart melted a little. 'Thanks. I was very tall as a teen, therefore I didn't conform with the others.'

'What a load of twaddle.'

Nick certainly knew how to make her feel good. But then so had her ex, until he'd got what he wanted, then he went into bully mode and never stopped. Not that she was saying Nick was bully material, only that she'd learned to be ultra cautious when it came to getting to know people. Might as well get it all out of the way. 'I was also married to a prize jerk who believed I was there to do as he wished all the time.'

'You left him?'

'Yes. There was only so much of his crap I

could take. I deserved a lot better.' Always would. Be warned. Not that Nick seemed at all interested in her, other than as a colleague, something to be grateful about, but it was hard to raise that emotion. Especially when he was standing only a few feet away, his tall frame making her feel warm and happy. Like they were a match. It would be too easy to reach out and touch him.

She spun away and snatched up the medicine kit to put on board. Time to get to work. To focus on reality, not daydreams. She was not touching Nick.

He was standing beside her, looking impressed. 'You're tough. Go you.'

Tough enough to keep her hands to herself? Tugging her shoulders back, she said, 'I had to be.'

Have to be if I'm going to keep my heart safe.

Heart? That was going too far. Being attracted to Nick did not mean she was falling for him. No way.

But her head would not shut up. Its next question was, *Surely not every man you're attracted to will turn out to be a bully?* Definitely not, but how was she to know who to trust? Men didn't come with referrals.

Joy stood in the doorway. 'You're both here already. That's good because we have a prem birth with complications needing retrieving and tak-

ing down to Brisbane ASAP. It was called in by
Dr Jones five minutes ago.'

'Matilda's mum, right?' Hopefully someone
was with Matilda while her mother was seeing
to her patient.

'Yes. The woman's at her clinic, it's been arranged for the ambulance to take her to the air-
field when I let her know you're on your way.'

'Let's do it.' Leesa headed out to the plane
where Darren was already waiting, ready to go.
It was good to have something to think about
other than her partner. Work partner. *Gorgeous
partner*, added a cheeky part of her mind.

It was true. Nick was awesome. And not for
her. The idea of a full-on relationship gave her
warm fuzzies—and chilly shivers. Being single
had its advantages. She didn't get told what to do
all the time, could make her own decisions and
stick to them—or dump them, whichever suited.

It could also be lonely not having that special
person who was hers, at her side. Family and
friends were great. Having a man to share the
big and little decisions, the fun and not-so-fun
moments, would be even better.

Nick was right beside her, case notes in hand
and wearing an expression that said he was men-
tally running through the equipment they'd need
and what was in the drug kit.

She nudged him. 'Everything's on board.'

'I know, but old habits don't go away.'

'They're the best.' She trotted up the stairs. 'Hey, Darren.'

'Morning you two. No rest for the wicked, eh?'

'You think?' Leesa gave a snort. If only she could have a bit of wicked in her life. Her gaze flicked over her shoulder to Nick as he closed them in. It might be better if they got down and dirty and she could get this craving for him out of her system. Yeah, nah. Best not. Disappointment filled her. But she could only laugh at herself. This was out there crazy.

Get over the guy.

Like it had worked last time.

'Can I take a front seat ride?' Nick asked Darren. 'I won't hold you up or get in the way.'

'Help yourself. I've already started take off procedures. Just get buckled in pronto.'

'Thanks, mate.'

Darren spoke to the control tower and the props began turning on one side of the plane, and then the other. 'Here we go. You'll get a clearer idea of the layout of the land from up above,' he told Nick, who was strapping himself in.

Leesa stretched her legs out in front of her. Great. Now she'd have all the air back here to herself.

'Do you want to read the notes?' Nick leaned back to her. 'There's not a lot to see.'

'Sure.' She took the paper he held out and shivered when their fingers collided. The man was a permanent fire sparkler with how he always set her alight. His hands were firm but gentle, hot while sensuous. Another shiver tripped down her back as she recalled them touching her. What she wouldn't do to share her bed with him again.

Biting her lip, she stared at the page in front of her. The words blurred as heat filled her. *Blink, blink. Swallow.* Her lungs filled, emptied.

The page slowly became clearer. Lucy Crosby, thirty-two, thirty-one weeks' gestation, had gone into labour at five that morning. Baby was born at six ten hours, was put into a ventilator and all functions were being monitored continuously. Mother had lost a significant amount of blood, and needed a transfusion on arrival at the designated hospital in Brisbane.

A glance at her watch told her the baby was barely an hour old. 'Come on, get cracking, there's a baby needing to be in the NICU.'

'We're airborne,' Darren replied through the headset.

'Oops, sorry, didn't mean to speak out loud.'

Both men laughed. 'Typical,' added Nick. 'But I know what you mean. These flying machines don't go fast enough sometimes.'

'This one will,' Darren sounded as though he'd been challenged.

Leesa watched the airport grow smaller as they rose quickly and listened to Nick's deep husky voice through her headphones. He could talk about paint drying on walls and she'd still be riveted. How pathetic was that? Definitely time to get out amongst it and find a guy to have some fun with. Not the one sitting in the right-hand seat up front. He'd be a lot of fun, but she feared he might snag her heart when she wasn't looking and that was not up for grabs. Not until she knew him very well anyway, because that was the only way to be safe. Besides, if she got Joy's job, she'd have to keep him at a distance.

'Leesa, can you set up the monitors while I get a needle into Alphie for fluids?' Nick leaned over the incubator. The little guy weighed fourteen hundred and twenty grams. It seemed an impossible number to survive, but he knew Alphie had every chance of putting on weight over the coming days as long as they got him to the intensive care unit ASAP.

'Onto it. His breathing's shallow and a little faster,' she said calmly.

'That's changed since we loaded him. I'll put a mask on him before anything else.'

'What's happening?' demanded the distraught father from the cockpit. He wasn't happy being there. He wanted to be with his son and wife.

Leesa looked up. 'Nick's going to help Alphie's breathing by putting an oxygen mask over his face. It won't hurt him at all.'

'What's wrong with his breathing? It was all right back at Dr Jones's.'

Nick carefully tightened the band around the baby's head just enough to keep it in place and turned to James. 'His breaths are coming a bit quick. I can't see anything else wrong with him.' He glanced at Leesa who nodded.

'BP's normal, heart rate good.'

Even though he expected that, Nick still felt relieved. These cases could go wrong very fast. This was when he was more than glad to have Leesa alongside him. Her competence was awesome.

'Can you check on Lucy?' Nick asked Leesa. The woman had haemorrhaged after giving birth, and while the bleeding had slowed, it hadn't stopped. Dr Jones had sutured the external tears but there was a serious internal wound that would see Lucy on her way to Theatre the moment she got to hospital.

'Onto it.' Leesa's smile warmed him through and through. At the moment they were a team, nothing else mattered other than getting their patients to hospital and giving them both all the care possible on the way. Would it be possible to get along just as well outside the job? It would be wonderful if they did, if he could give in to his feelings with no fear for his heart.

'Lucy, how are you doing?' Leesa asked. 'I'm going to check the bleeding.'

'Don't worry about me. Look after Alphie,' the woman whispered.

'Alphie's in good hands. Nick's watching over him like a hawk.'

His heart expanded at Leesa's words. She knew how to make him feel good. 'Alphie's doing great. He's a tough wee man. You need to be looked after, too.'

'Alphie needs you, Lucy,' James called from the front.

'It doesn't feel right to take your attention away from my baby,' Lucy said.

Leesa nodded. 'I understand, but your boy doesn't need two of us right now, whereas you need some help.' She snapped on fresh gloves. 'Let's get you sorted. You want to be cleaned up before we arrive at the hospital.'

Again, Leesa was being patient. Nick sighed. She was hard to ignore. Impossible, in fact. But he'd keep trying—until he couldn't any more. Which wasn't far off.

Darren raised his beer to everyone round the table, those not on duty who were at the pub down the road from the airport. 'Here's to the end of another week.'

'All right for some.' Leesa tapped her bottle against his and then everyone else's. 'I'm on all weekend.'

'Yes, and we know you love it.' Nick gave her a return tap.

It was true. She loved her job. Had even enjoyed working with the new doctor on the days they'd been rostered together. More than enjoyed. He was great company and just as sexy when he was being serious as he was when he was away from work. 'Most of the time I do.'

Nick looked surprised. 'Most? I'd have said all the time.'

'No job is that perfect.' She'd put her hand up to cover call this weekend because she wanted to be busy. It was the first anniversary of when her best friend was involved in a car versus bus accident that she didn't survive. It had been hard for everyone, especially her husband. John wasn't coping at all, to the point he'd been temporarily stood down from working as an aircraft engineer.

She looked around for him, having seen him with a couple of engineers when she'd arrived. He was leaning on the far end of the bar looking lost. She'd keep an eye on him and probably join him shortly. In the meantime, she'd focus on her workmates. This unwinding time was important for everyone after a week dealing with some heart-wrenching cases. Turning to Nick, she asked. 'What are you up to this weekend?'

Nick shrugged. 'Haven't planned anything really.'

'Sounds dull.'

'Not really.'

Strange how at work he talked more easily, but when they were away from work he seemed to go quiet. Just with her? No, he hadn't been very chatty with anyone. 'Have you ever come up this far north before?'

'No, never. It is a long way from anywhere,' he replied.

Hadn't she heard that before? 'Come on. We've got an airport. An international one to boot.'

'I've mostly spent my time in the large cities. This is a new experience for me.' Finally, a smile came her way. Plus a few more words. 'I do need to get out and see more of Oz, don't I?'

'I reckon.'

I'd make a good tour guide.

So much for keeping her distance. Thankfully she hadn't put that out there. Nick didn't need to know what she'd thought. Not that he'd be likely to take her up on the offer, he seemed as intent on keeping his distance as she was.

'I hear the Daintree's a great place to visit.'

'Watch out for the crocs,' she laughed. 'There

are plenty of warning signs around the area, but still.'

'So, you want me back at work next week?' He grinned, making her head feel light.

Damn him. He did that too easily. 'Maybe.'

His grin remained fixed in place.

And she continued to feel light headed. Time to move away and get her mental feet back on the ground. She'd check on John and come back to the gang shortly.

'I'll be back,' Leesa said before heading over to the bar and hugging a man staring into the depths of his glass.

Nick sipped his beer and listened to the conversation going on around him at the table. They were a great bunch to work with. This past week had highlighted the reason he'd moved yet again. New faces, new challenges as far as the job went. Nothing exciting about the new apartment, but that was normal. Time to buy his own place? Thanks to Patrick he was very lucky not to have a student loan hanging over his head. Buying a house suggested permanence, something he longed for. Here? In Cairns, where Leesa lived? The million-dollar question.

'You hear Joy's handed her notice in?' said Carl, another doctor working for the same outfit as him.

'When did she do that?' Darren asked.

Nick was intrigued. Only a couple of hours ago Joy was telling him how pleased she was with the way he was fitting in. Not a word about her leaving had passed her lips, but he was the new boy on the block.

'A few days ago, apparently. She's not leaving for a couple of months, and then she and her husband are going to tour Europe for an indefinite period.'

'Does that mean her job's up for grabs? Or have management already got someone lined up?' asked Jess, a nurse he'd worked with yesterday.

Carl shrugged. 'Joy only said she was going to talk to the staff about it next week. No idea what that means, but could be they're looking for a replacement amongst you medics.'

Interest flared in Nick. He could apply. If he was going to settle down it would be perfect. It might help him stay grounded as it wouldn't be as easy to walk away.

Leesa.

It would mean no getting away from her. But did he really want to? His gaze strayed across the room to that tall, beautiful woman who had somehow managed to start him thinking of a future he'd believed impossible. Hard to imagine not seeing her every day. But did that fit in with her being the one person who'd find him lovable enough to stay around for ever?

Leesa was holding the man's hand. Her head was close to his. She appeared to be talking quietly.

Nick's stomach dropped. It was one thing to hug a guy, but to hold his hand? No, there was more to this. Those two were acting like they had something going on. Yet she hadn't raced over to him when she arrived.

Just then the man ran his other hand down the side of his face, and Nick's mouth soured. He wore a wedding band. Married, and Leesa was holding his hand. He could not abide by that.

Leesa wasn't his girlfriend, but to see her with a married man like that had the warning bells clanging. Here he'd been thinking she might be the woman who could help him turn his world around. Wrong. His ex hadn't been honest with him, which was why he had to be able to trust whoever he fell in love with, when it happened. *If* it happened, and that had started to look possible—until now. Or was he over reacting? There could be a perfectly sane explanation. This was Leesa, after all.

'Want another beer?' Carl asked.

'No, thanks. I'm heading away.' Sitting here seeing Leesa getting all close and tender with that man was doing his head in. He'd been mistaken about her. All those sensations that heated his body, that had him looking at her, were a joke. She wasn't his type at all. He had to stick to dating women who were honest about their wish to have fun with no expectations about the future. Far safer that way. Except it was hard to believe Leesa would be dishonest about a relationship. But how well did he know her?

'Hey, I'll see you all at work.' Leesa stood at the table.

How had he missed her approaching? She sure didn't look guilty about anything.

She was still talking. 'I'm giving John a lift home. He's had a few too many to drive.'

'He's not looking great,' Darren noted.

'He's not in good shape,' Leesa agreed. 'It's the one-year anniversary.'

'Sure he's going to be all right home alone?' Carl asked.

'His father's staying the night. He was meant to be here but got held up at work and has gone straight to the house.' Leesa glanced Nick's way. 'John's wife passed a year ago tomorrow. She was my best friend.'

Guilt tore through him. How could he have immediately suspected the worst? Why hadn't he waited to find out what was going on before jumping to the wrong conclusion? Went to show how screwed up he was. How much Ellie's betrayal had affected him. Still did, apparently.

He wanted to move on, to create a happy, loving life while denying anyone near his heart. There was a lot to put behind him for that to work. 'Leesa, I'm really sorry to hear that.' In more ways than she could imagine. 'It's not going to be an easy day for you either.' Hence, she'd opted to work. She must be hurting big time. 'Who else is on tomorrow?'

Carl put his hand up. 'Going to miss my wife's first golf competition.' He laughed. 'Might be a blessing in disguise.'

'How about I cover for you?' Nick suggested. He could be with Leesa if she wanted to talk about her friend, or support her silently if that suited.

'You serious? I owe you, Nick. Cheers.'

'No problem.' Unless Leesa wasn't happy with him, but he'd deal with that if it arose.

Darren stood up. 'Leesa, I'll come with you out to the car.'

'Thanks.' Leesa's face was grim. 'I'm hoping John's all right for the ride home.' She headed back to her friend.

'Poor bugger,' Carl said as he drained his bottle. 'Sure you don't want another?'

'No, thanks.' He stood up. Leesa was worried about her passenger. He'd offer to go with them. It was the least he could do for jumping to the wrong conclusion. His medical skills might be useful. Leesa wouldn't be worried without reason.

Leesa and Darren walked past with John between them. Leesa held the man's arm as he staggered.

Following them out to her car, he got a surprised look from Leesa. 'Thought I'd take a ride with you in case your friend needs help.'

'You don't have to do that.' She sounded snappy, but the relief in her eyes suggested she'd be glad of some help. He wasn't in the habit of jumping to conclusions, except when it came to trusting people not to let him down, so it only showed how much Leesa was getting under his skin. She was special, and he couldn't get past that. 'Not really. I'll sit in the back as the front might be best for John in his condition.'

John appeared to be past hearing what was going on. Not a good look.

'It'll be a slow trip but we don't have far to go,' Leesa said as Darren helped John into the car. 'Hopefully his dad will be there by the time we arrive.'

'We can wait with him if not.'

Leesa glanced at him in the rear-view mirror. 'Thank you.'

'Where do you want me to drop you off? At work to pick up your ute or the apartment?' Leesa asked Nick, who was looking very comfortable in the front seat of her car. Despite all the warnings in her head, she couldn't deny how much she enjoyed his company at work and at play. Though there hadn't been any play so far, and might never be if she managed to keep her wits about her, which was proving difficult.

John's father had been waiting for them and, after they'd got John inside and sprawled over the couch, Nick had given him a quick check over. 'Sleep and a bucket at the ready is all I can recommend. Too much to drink and probably little or no food all day,' was his conclusion.

'Happening too often,' his father had muttered. 'He refuses to get help. Apart from tying him to the back of my truck there's nothing I can do.'

She'd hugged John, her own sadness at losing Danielle feeling heavier than usual. She missed her so much, it was almost unreal. No wonder John wasn't coping. Danielle had been the love of his life. Still was.

'The apartment's fine.' Nick brought her back to the here and now. 'Why don't you come up for a bite to eat? I'll order something in. You look done in, Leesa.'

She'd love nothing more than to sit down with him and not talk a lot, just relax in each other's company. 'I can't. I've got to pick up Baxter and take him for his walk. He'll be thinking his throat's cut since dinner hasn't arrived in his bowl.'

'Can I join you? Fresh air would be good for me too. We could stop for some food afterwards and take it back to my apartment. Baxter's welcome to join us.' Nick said.

It was impossible to fight the need to spend time with him right now. It was too hard when she was aching for her best friend. Good company would help ease the pain and, despite her misgivings about getting too involved, Nick was more than good company.

'You're welcome to,' she said.

At the dog care centre Baxter bounced around both of them as though he'd been imprisoned for a week.

'Freedom, eh, mate?' Nick rubbed his ears, making Leesa think she should bounce around too and get a few pats.

Baxter nuzzled in against Nick's leg, his tail wagging so fast Leesa figured it'd was about to fall off.

'He likes you. Let's go to the esplanade again. It's his favourite walk.' Hers too.

Once there, Nick threw a ball for Baxter to race after and bring back.

'I like you doing that. I don't cover half the distance when I throw it and Baxter doesn't get so worn out.'

Baxter dropped the ball in front of Nick and

sat back, waiting impatiently for him to throw it again.

'As long as it doesn't go into the water,' Nick hurled the ball. 'A wet dog in the car would make me unpopular.'

'There're plenty of towels in the boot. Anyway, what's the point of having a dog if I can't deal with the odd mess to clean up?'

'I agree.'

'Have you ever had a dog? Or a pet of any sort?' He was so good with her boy, he seemed to understand what Baxter wanted.

'Never.'

The usual shutdown when she asked about his personal life. 'Ever consider it?'

'Sometimes, but I'm not home enough.'

No family, no pets. Friends? Best avoid that one. 'I mightn't have taken in Baxter if I hadn't known Karin. She's amazing, looking after him out of hours when I'm caught up with work. Mum and Dad take him if I'm really stuck, that's his favourite place to go to.'

'Gets spoiled rotten?'

'Totally. We always had a dog when I was growing up, but now Mum's got Parkinson's she's unwilling to get another as the day will come when she can't look after it. Dad disagrees but she won't budge on her decision, says having Baxter some days is enough. I think it's part of her way of coping with the Parkinson's.'

'I bet that's hard for both your parents.'

'A complete game changer. Mum mostly tries to carry on as she always has, but she did a lot of work on the farm driving tractors, fixing fences, you name it, and now she's had to give all that up. She was also a crack amateur golfer. I know there are days she can't deal with things, but she never lets Kevin, my brother, or I see it. Sometimes Dad talks to us about how he feels, but mostly he keeps it to himself.'

Not always the way to go, as things got bottled up, but Dad had taken up golf himself in the last year. While nowhere near as good as Mum, he said hitting the ball for as far as possible was a great way to let the frustrations go.

'How long has she had the disease?'

'About eighteen months. It was the main reason I came home. Not to hang around being a pest, but to support Ma and Pa as and when they need it. Besides, I can't imagine not being here. They're my family and that means everything to me.'

Nick took her hand and swung it between them as they walked along. 'I'm glad for you.'

Glancing sideways she saw a wistful look in his eyes. She wanted to tell him he could have that too if he really wanted it, but she suspected he already knew. From the little she'd learned she wondered what held him back from putting himself out there to find the special person to go through life with. 'Your family life wasn't so wonderful?' Her fingers tightened around his.

'No.' He dropped her hand, looking shocked he'd taken it in the first place.

'I'm sorry to hear that.' She took his hand back, and held him lightly.

The relaxed feeling when he'd first taken her hand had gone, replaced by a stiffness that told her to leave the subject alone. And him. If only he would talk, then he might get some of the angst off his chest and feel a little freer. Of course, she'd possibly misinterpreted his reaction to her question, but she didn't think so.

They were a right mixed-up pair: she wanting to settle down with a great guy while still nervous about him turning out to be all wrong for her, and Nick shutting down every time family was mentioned. How would he react if she asked him to join her for dinner tomorrow? He'd probably laugh at her and remind her he'd already turned her down once this week. Best not ask. She called Baxter and turned around to head back to the car, Nick quiet beside her.

Baxter seemed to sense something wasn't quite right, trotting beside Nick all the way, totally ignoring her. It'd be funny if it didn't make her a little peeved. He was her boy, but truly she was happy he was looking out for her friend. If only she knew which buttons to press that'd make Nick relax as much with her. 'What do you feel like for dinner?' she asked. Then laughed. 'Not you, Baxter. You'll have the dried food that's in the car.'

'I don't get to share that?' Nick asked with a wry smile.

Leesa relaxed. They were back to normal, for now at least. 'Maybe.'

'I'm covering for Carl tomorrow,' Nick said quietly.

Forget normal. Her stomach knotted at the thought of more time together. It *would* be a diversion from thinking too much about Danielle. Sure thing. Funny how she could hear her friend laughing at her.

Go, girlfriend.

CHAPTER FOUR

FAMILY. IT WAS a big deal with Leesa. It was a big deal for him too, but from a completely different perspective, Nick acknowledged as he set the Thai takeout containers on the outdoor table. She had what he'd only dreamed of since his grandfather had passed. What he'd been looking for, yet afraid to give it all he had after Ellie did her number on him. Ellie had been the final straw.

He might've jumped into their marriage too fast, all because he wanted love and family so much that he hadn't stopped and really listened to Ellie and what she wanted. But he had learned a lesson. Listen to his head and heart. They had to be in agreement and, looking back, he saw that might not have been the case with Ellie.

Seemed the time had come to let go of the past and move on. If only he knew how do it safely. The idea of being hurt again made him shiver, while thinking it might all be worth the risk if it meant he could be happy. As Patrick said, 'Life's too short to waste it.'

'Want a glass for your beer?' the woman making him rethink a lot of things asked.

Shaking his head, he reached for the bottle she held out. 'It's fine as it is.' Then, before he could change his mind, he said, 'I was married once. It was a complete failure.'

Leesa studied him briefly. 'I know what that's like.'

'Yes, you do. My wife was unfaithful.' Among a few other things. But he'd said more than enough for now. 'Baxter doesn't seem fazed being five storeys off the ground.' The dog was peering between the balustrades at the street below, his tail wagging hard as he spied two dogs.

Leesa stared at him, then nodded. 'He's usually okay with any situation as long as I'm around.' Leesa rubbed her pet's ears. 'Aren't you, boy?'

'Can you give me the details of where you got him from? I think I'd like to get a dog, after all.' It was a sudden decision and yet it felt right. Another step towards settling down.

Another? Try the first. So far everything had been ideas, nothing fixed in reality. Warmth spread through him at the thought of having a pet. He'd never had one before. What the hell was going on? Swigging a mouthful of beer, he glanced at Leesa, and knew she was changing him, whether he liked it or not. Truly, he did like it. Even when he was coming up with reasons not to.

'I'll text you the website address.' She had her phone out and was tapping away. 'I'll recommend you to Karin as she's very protective of the rescue dogs, she usually wants so much background that it can take for ever, unless she knows the person giving a reference.'

'Cheers. It'll have to be a dog that can handle living without a backyard to play in. In the beginning anyway.'

'Lots of walks make up for that. There's also the dog care centre Karin runs for when you're at work.'

He'd seen the big yard there and the dogs running around pretty much nonstop. 'I'd be happy to use that service. I do not want to leave any dog of mine locked inside the apartment alone all day while I'm out.' This was getting serious. None of the usual back-off feelings were in sight. Exciting really.

Leesa opened the containers and sniffed the air like she hadn't eaten for a week. 'Everything smells delicious.'

'Dive in.'

She didn't need a second invitation. Rice and stir-fried vegetables were piling up on her plate, followed by chicken red curry. 'Thanks for this.'

'Anytime.' He meant it. Despite his resistance

she was becoming a part of his outside work life. He couldn't imagine not sharing a meal or going for a walk with her and Baxter—and the dog he would get. Quite an ordinary lifestyle by all accounts, and one he had little experience of. One he would like almost more than anything else. Love would be the deal breaker to being beyond wonderful.

'It's nice just sitting and relaxing. I worry about John a lot. He needs help with his grief but won't listen to anyone about doing something about it.'

'He's not alone with that. People don't like admitting they're not coping. How long were they married?'

'Two and a half years. They were so happy it was unbelievable. I admit to occasionally having been a bit jealous. Then Danielle died and it seemed they'd been cramming in as much as possible before tragedy struck.' She looked at him with a wonky smile. 'Sounds crazy I know but…'

'Hardly crazy. No one knows what's around the corner. They say we should grab everything we can while it's possible.'

Listen to yourself. You haven't exactly been following that advice.

'Danielle was always a bit that way, getting involved with sports, theatre and her career as a pilot. Sometimes I wondered how she fitted in her marriage, but they always seemed happy and there wasn't a moment they weren't doing something they enjoyed.' Leesa was staring out over the railing, sadness filling her face. 'I miss her so much.'

Nick couldn't help himself. He got up and crossed to her, lifting her up and wrapping her in his arms to hug her tight. His chin rested on her head as she snuggled closer. The scent of antiseptic and roses tickled his nostrils. He smiled. Reality was never quite as romantic as it was made out to be, but he liked that about being with Leesa. Reality was key to what he wanted in the future and, if it came packaged in this amazing woman, he could be ready to leap forward with her.

If she'd have him. But he was getting ahead of himself. This moment was about Leesa and her grief, not his heart. Though that was definitely getting more involved every day. 'One day at a time, eh?' He wasn't sure what he was referring to—Leesa's grief or his optimism.

'Only way to go.' She leaned back in his arms and looked at him. 'Thank you for being here for me. I don't usually let anyone see how I'm feeling.'

Everything inside him softened. Leesa was sharing herself with *him*. It meant a lot. 'I'm glad I was able to help.'

Her eyes brightened, tugging at his heart in an unfamiliar way, which was becoming too familiar. 'Funny how we seem to understand each other so easily.'

'Like that night we met in the park when we seemed to click.' Did she understand he wanted to kiss her? Leaning in, his lips touched hers.

Her answer was to open her mouth under his and push her tongue inside, tasting him, winding him up so tight, so fast he felt as if his body would explode. 'Leesa,' he groaned into her.

She pressed her full length hard up against him. Those amazing breasts he still remembered flattened against his chest, her hips rocked against his, as she continued to kiss him with a passion that was mind-blowing.

He'd missed this, missed Leesa as he'd known her those few nights. Her buttocks were under his palms and turned him on even more. Hot, soft, sexy as. He was so hard he ached. 'Leesa?'

'Yes, Nick.' Her fingers were working at his trouser zip, making a job of what should be easy.

'Let me.' He wouldn't last if she didn't hurry.

'Uh, uh.' A couple of fingers slid under his trousers, hot on his abdomen.

Too hot. He pulled back. 'Slow down or I won't be there for you.'

'Can't have that.' She removed her hand so damned slowly those hot fingertips worked magic on his skin, sending his blood racing downward.

He had to bite down hard to hold himself together. 'Stop.'

'Can't do that either.' Her tongue ran over her lips.

'Come on. Inside.' He wouldn't make it to his bed, but there was a large sofa in the lounge.

She must've had the same thought because she headed directly for it, pulling him with her.

Not that he needed any encouragement.

Then she dropped his hand to pull her shirt over her head.

His mouth dried. His memory had failed him. She was so beautiful it hurt to breathe. Her breasts filled their lace cups perfectly. Her skin was creamy and soft, just as his dreams kept reminding him. He had to have her. Now.

No. That's not how this played out. Leesa came first.

'Nick.'

His name whispered against his mouth felt so sexy he nearly exploded.

'Condom,' she whispered.

'What?'

'Condom.'

Yikes. Showed how far gone he was. 'Be right back.' So much for the bedroom being too far away. They had to be careful, no matter how they were feeling.

He pulled the drawer so hard it hit the floor. At least the packet he needed was at the top.

Back to Leesa, who was sprawled over the sofa watching him as he raced towards her, his erection leading the way.

'Give me that.' She tugged the packet from his lifeless fingers and tore it open with her teeth. Then she reached for him, slid her hand down his length, squeezed softly, slid up again.

A breath stalled in the back of his throat. Lowering onto the sofa beside her exquisite body he found her wet heat. Ran a finger over her, and when she bucked under his touch, he did it again. And again. And again. He kept stroking her, drowning in her cries of ecstasy until she cried out and fell back, her eyes wide and her chest rising and falling fast. 'Nick,' she croaked.

Then she was up on an elbow, reaching for him, sliding the condom over his shaft so slowly he couldn't breathe for the heat and tension gripping him. 'Leesa, stop or I'll come.'

Her smile undid him. He tensed and then she was under him, guiding him inside, and he was joining her as she arched up into him. They were together. Completely.

Leesa stretched her whole body. She felt tender all over, and so relaxed and happy. Making out with Dr Sexy had been just what she needed. Hearing a rumbling sound coming from the man himself, she laughed. 'Hungry by any chance?'

'That was quite a work out,' he grinned and kissed her forehead. 'Seriously, thank you. I enjoyed every moment.' He'd said thank you in a note after the first time. Pretty amazing that a man could openly thank her for being so intimate.

'I did too.' She hadn't had sex since their fling in Cairns, hadn't wanted to. Every time she thought that she should put some effort into finding a special man to start the life she longed for, memories of Nick and their lovemaking would stop her in her tracks. He had been wonderful and would be a hard, if not impossible, act to follow. Those few nights had meant so much. There'd been a depth to being with Nick—she knew she'd never settle for less again.

He was getting up. 'I'll get us some food.'

'It'll need heating up. Can I grab a quick shower while you're doing that?' She hadn't had one before leaving work and was more than ready for one now.

'Go for it. Towels are in the large drawer beneath the basin.'

She hadn't even stepped under the water when Nick came through the bathroom door, roaring with laughter. 'Forget the Thai. Seems Baxter's into rice and stir fry. There's curry but it's on the deck, so guess he wasn't keen on that. He's got a very round stomach at the moment.'

'The little brat. I was looking forward to more. It's been ages since I had Thai.' She laughed. 'That'll teach me for being so easily side-tracked.'

'Can't blame him. We kind of neglected him.' Nick had his phone out. 'I'll order some more. Handy that they're only a few doors along the road.'

'I'll have my shower.'

'I'll join you in a moment.'

No food, but having Nick wash her back was going to be just as good. And the food wouldn't be too long. Quite the night.

And it only got better.

Just after midnight Leesa crawled out of Nick's bed and dragged on her clothes. 'I'm on duty at seven, and I need to take Baxter home so Mum can pick him up later in the morning.'

'We both probably need some shut eye. I'll see you down to your car.'

It was cool that he wanted to make certain she was safe. Not that she had any concerns, but still, Nick was a gentleman through and through. What's more, she really liked that about him. It was a first. Not even in the first months of their relationship had Connor been so kind. Nick was nothing like him, hadn't shown any tendency towards bullying, and by now she did have experience to fall back on. She could start to trust her instincts.

After getting Baxter settled on the back seat, she turned to Nick and gave him a quick kiss. 'I've had a great time.'

'Me too.'

She was free tomorrow night to do it again. And the next one.

Don't rush things.

Good idea. Let the excitement and thrill of earlier settle a bit before making rash decisions.

On a sorry indrawn breath, she said, 'See you at work. Unless you want me to come by and pick you up, since your ute's still at the airport?'

'I'll grab a taxi.' Withdrawing already? Or saving her the hassle of having to go across town?

She'd run with that. It felt better. She had to stop looking for trouble and get on with having fun with a decent man. Nick was more than decent. He was sexy as all be it. He was so good looking she wanted to keep prodding him to make sure he was for real. His love making was beyond reality. She lost herself completely when he touched her. Maybe she did need to back off fast until her head was clear, so she could think carefully about where to go from here. 'No problem.' Clambering into the car, she headed for home, and time to dream about the hours she'd spent with Nick.

* * *

Leesa spent most of the rest of the night reflecting on Nick and their relationship. Whenever she closed her eyes, he was there behind her eyelids, smiling, laughing, being kind, gentle. And not giving much away.

Winding her up tight all over again, only this time it was all about her feelings and what to do about them. He was growing on her fast. Too fast, when she wanted to take one slow step at a time. She'd fallen for Connor quickly and look where that led. Part of her, a big part, wanted to let all that go so she could trust Nick. He really was nothing like her ex. Not in any way.

She was getting ahead of herself. There'd been nothing in their hours together to say that he might be interested in her, other than for a good time in the sack.

Now she was heading into work just as she had been a year ago when she got the call to say Danielle was gone. Her fingers whitened on the steering wheel. 'Miss you something terrible, girlfriend.' Would she ever get over losing Danielle? In some ways she probably would, but in others never. 'Damn it, Danielle, I need to talk to you, to hear you give me a speech about how, because I was a moron over Connor, it doesn't mean it'll happen again.'

Had Nick taken Carl's shift to be with her on

the day she was mourning her friend? She suspected so. It would be second nature for him. Turning into the airport, she drove slowly towards the Flying Health Care hangar. She should be buzzing after last night, but now she suddenly felt nothing but trepidation. What if she was making a fool of herself with Nick? Everyone here seemed to think he was a great guy, but that wasn't a reason to fall in love with him. For her that had to be all about trust. The thing was, she did trust him. So why the hesitation?

'Morning, Leesa,' Nick called when she walked into the hangar. He was at the cupboard checking the drug kit they took on board. He didn't stop what he was doing to give her a smile or acknowledge the night before. Having similar doubts as her? Quite likely, considering he had some family issues.

'Hi, there,' she replied. 'How's things?'

'All good.'

Not super chatty. But when was he? When they were sitting on his deck eating Thai and getting hot and bothered. That's when. She shook her head and headed to the locker room, walking away from the temptation of wrapping her arms around him, along with a quick kiss. It wouldn't be professional to do that here. She probably shouldn't follow up on last night either, not when he seemed to have gone quiet on her.

Instead, she went to see if they had any flights arranged. Saturdays were usually quieter but she hoped today would be an exception.

'We're giving Jacob a lift home at eleven.'

She nearly leapt out of her skin at the sound of Nick's voice right behind her. So much for thinking he was keeping to himself. 'I didn't know he was still down here. He'll be fretting about his friend's birthday present.'

'Apparently, he had a rough time after his chemo and was kept in PICU for two days. He's doing all right now, but it's likely to happen again as the chemo takes its toll.'

'It will.' The build-up of the treatment always had a long-term effect, which she hated seeing with her patients. Especially the little ones. Being a parent was on her wish list, and it seemed nothing but exciting from where she stood, but she knew all too well that wasn't always the case. She did know, if she was lucky enough to become a mother, she'd love her kid to bits and be super strong for him or her no matter what.

'At the moment there's nothing else on our schedule,' Nick informed her. 'I'm putting the jug on. Feel like a tea or coffee?'

'Tea, thanks. Is Darren here?'

'Doing his aircraft checks. He'll be in shortly.' Nick turned towards the kitchen.

Definitely not overly friendly. But she hadn't

put herself out to be chirpy either. It was still hard not to rush over and hug him, to feel his long strong body against her.

The main phone rang sharply. Racing to answer it, she silently begged for a job so she didn't have to sit around in the kitchen for hours. 'Flying Health Care. Leesa speaking.'

'Hey, Leesa, it's Michael. We've got a call from Weipa to pick up a man who's been in a truck versus car accident. Internal injuries, fractures to both legs and pelvis.' Michael worked the phones for emergency services. 'I'll adjust the flight time for Jacob to early afternoon.'

Poor Jacob. Things weren't panning out for him this week. 'Right. On our way.' She hung up, feeling guilty. A seriously injured patient wasn't quite what she meant as a distraction. 'Forget the tea and coffee, Nick. We're on.'

'What've we got?'

Moving quickly to the plane, she filled him in on the scant facts. Once they were on the way more would come through on the laptop they took with them. 'Jacob's flight will be delayed until we're back.'

'He won't be happy about that. He so wanted to see his friend and give him his present. I imagine every hour is going to seem like another day to him.' Nick gave her a brief smile.

A smile that touched her, and loosened some

of her worries about them, despite it disappearing almost as soon as he'd produced it. 'You're not wrong there.'

'Why doesn't he go by car? It's only about three hours, isn't it?'

'Jacob gets car sick, and add in the chemo effects and it wouldn't be pleasant for anyone,' Leesa told him as she waved bye to the ground crew pulling the stairs away from the plane.

'Yet he's fine in the plane.' Nick buckled into his seat. 'But that's how it is for some.'

'Ready back here,' she told Darren through the headset she'd pulled on.

'It's going to be a bit bumpy over the hills,' the pilot warned them.

'No problem.' She didn't mind minor turbulence. It was a different story when they had a patient on board, as it added to the stress and pain for that person, and made helping them difficult as they had to remain strapped in their seats.

Nick had the laptop open and was reading the information about the patient they were flying to Weipa to pick up. 'Not looking good.'

'Fill me in.'

'Fractured ribs, both femurs, and right upper arm. Suspected perforated lung. Swelling in the abdomen so there must be more injuries in that area. We're going to be pushing it to get him to Cairns without a major problem occurring.'

'Going as fast as allowed,' Darren came through the headset.

'I figured you might be,' Nick responded. Then he looked her way. 'You good to go with whatever happens?'

'Always.' As if he had to ask. It was the nature of the job to be prepared for worst-case scenarios. They happened often enough for her to know wishful thinking didn't prevent them.

'You won't get a better paramedic than Leesa,' Darren said a little sharply.

'Thanks, Darren.' Turning to Nick, she removed the mouthpiece so Darren didn't hear. 'Do not question my ability. I am well versed in the medical requirements of our work.'

'I'm sorry. It was a reflex question. I don't doubt your medical skills.'

'Thank you.' They had moved on from their intimate night to being tense with each other. Not a good look for the future. Better to know now than later.

She turned to face out the window for the rest of the flight.

Nick knew he'd stuffed up big time. The anger in Leesa's expression told him she wasn't going to forgive him any time soon for questioning her ability to deal with the death of a patient. It had been a mistake. He hadn't deliberately set out to check she was comfortable with what might lie ahead, he'd been speaking aloud in an attempt to discuss what they might face. Except it came out as a question, and she was not happy with him.

Talk about going from a high to a low. Last night had been beyond fantastic. Making love with Leesa couldn't be better. She was so giving. And accepting. Almost loving. Almost. They were not falling in love. They couldn't. He wasn't ready, despite his feelings for her growing stronger by the day. After last night, it was going to be even harder to stay away from her.

Other than at work, and then they were professionals, looking after patients, keeping each other at arm's length. He was also about to apply for Joy's position, which meant he might have to take a step back to remain professional.

But right now, he wanted to reach out and touch Leesa, to tell her how much he believed in her medical skills. Other skills too. When it came to sticking up for herself, she was strong. She'd proved that by helping those women at the Brisbane base. There'd be no walking all over her, and he'd never want to. Leesa was his dream woman. His mind went back to last night when he was inside her and she was crying out as she came. More than a dream. She was real and near perfect, and he was still hesitant.

A while later she turned to look at him. 'Weipa's to our left. Darren must've had his foot to the pedal all the way.'

'No such thing as a pedal up here,' Darren retorted.

'Thank goodness for that or who knows how fast this plane might've gone.' Nick stretched his legs to loosen the kinks in his muscles. 'I've never been this far north and all I'm going to see is the airport.'

'Somewhere to come when you have leave to use up. Lots of people go through using four-wheel drive vehicles. I haven't done it, but know there's certain times of the year when it's safer. The rainy season's not one as the mud builds up and vehicles get bogged down. Not easy to get out when you're in the middle of nowhere.'

'Surely people go in groups?'

'Mostly, but there're always the exceptions. I remember one chopper flight we had to pick up a woman who'd had her leg broken when her husband revved the truck, it ran over her because it wasn't as stuck as he'd believed.'

Idiot. How could a man do that when his wife was in line with the vehicle? 'Lack of experience in the outback then.'

'Definitely.'

'Have you heard that Joy's leaving?' he asked. 'I'm thinking of applying for the position.'

'Me too.'

'That I didn't expect.'

'Why ever not? I'm as capable as anyone to do it justice,' she snapped, taken aback by the shock in his face.

'I know you are. It just never occurred to me you might want to run the outfit. You're so happy doing what you do.'

'I am, but there's nothing wrong with wanting to advance my career. Same as you want.'

'True.'

'It could prove interesting,' Leesa retorted as the wheels touched down on the tarmac and the plane slowed.

Unsure how she felt about his revelation, he moved on. 'There's an ambulance waiting by the shed. No, the driver's started backing towards where I presume Darren's going to park. A woman's already pushing the stairs this way.'

'They're obviously in a hurry. Not a good sign.' Unbuckling her belt, Leesa waited impatiently at the door for the plane to come to a halt, as near to the ambulance as possible without jeopardising anyone's safety.

'I agree.' Internal bleeding could lead to cardiac arrest. Or the man might've gone into a deep coma from a head wound. Worse, his lung might be compromised by a broken rib gouging a hole in it.

Stop. Wait for the facts before starting to work

out how to get this man to Cairns safely. 'I'd say we'll be back in the air in minutes, Darren.'

'Gotcha.'

'Here we go.' Leesa slid the door open as the plane stopped. The stairs were getting close.

They both grabbed a handle as the woman reached them and applied the brakes.

Nick leapt down the steps two at a time and strode to the ambulance as its back doors opened. 'Hi, I'm Nick, a doctor.'

'Hey, Nick. Heard we had someone new.' A woman began moving the trolley with their patient onto the tarmac. 'This is Maxwell O'Neill, forty-seven. Severe trauma to head, lungs, abdomen and legs. He suffered cardiac arrest fifteen minutes ago. We resuscitated him, but his heart rate's slow. Given the injuries blood loss is probably high.'

'Right, no hanging around then.'

Within minutes the stretcher was on the mini lift with Leesa at the man's side, pressing the button that made them rise up to the plane door. Nick shot up the stairs to help unload the stretcher onto the bed. He was barely aware of the plane lifting off as he read the monitors displaying Maxwell's heart reading, blood pressure and his breathing. 'This is going to be one long trip.' Every minute would feel like an hour as they worked to keep Maxwell alive.

Leesa looked up from where she was preparing the defibrillator in case Maxwell's heart stopped again. The chances were high. 'We can do it.' Her smile was small but warm, easing some of his tension.

It felt good to have her with him for this. She fed his confidence so that he did believe in himself. Not that he didn't usually, but there were some cases when he knew the odds were stacked against saving a patient—this was one of them. Having Leesa here took away some of that pressure. 'Thanks.'

Her reply was another smile.

So he was back in the good books—for now at least.

Thirty minutes later the line on the heart monitor flat-lined.

Leesa immediately placed the defib pads on Maxwell's bare chest and stepped back.

Nick pushed the button and waited, heart in his throat, for the electric current to get up to peek.

Maxwell's body lifted from the stretcher as the shock struck. Dropped back.

The air filled with a steady beeping sound.

Nick exhaled heavily. 'Phew. Thank goodness.'

Leesa wiped her brow. 'I can't believe his heart restarted at the first attempt.' There was a wobble in her voice.

'Hey, we were ready for it and wasted no time giving him a shock.'

'I know, but still.'

'Yeah, I get it.'

Twenty minutes out of Cairns it happened again. This time it took two shocks to get Maxwell's heart beating and the rhythm was all over the place.

Darren came through the headset. 'There's a helicopter on standby to take your patient to the hospital. There's been a crash on the main road and traffic's built up for kilometres either side.'

The last thing this man needed was a hold up. He probably wouldn't survive much longer without all the high-tech equipment only available in hospital. 'We'll go with him.'

'That's the plan,' Darren came back.

A thought came out of nowhere. 'Jacob's not going to be happy.'

Leesa glanced at him. 'I know. But we can pick him up in the chopper for the short hop back to the airport and the plane.'

Of course she'd think of that. 'Get onto whoever deals with these things and arrange it when you've got a free moment.'

'Tomorrow?' she laughed.

'Not if you want Jacob to still talk to you.'

'Good point.' Leesa grabbed a moment to call Michael and get Jacob and his mother's flight sorted.

CHAPTER FIVE

'SEE YOU NEXT TIME, Jacob,' Leesa waved at her favourite patient before heading out to the plane.

'Promise you will be here?' Jacob gave her a cheeky grin. He was happier than he'd been when he boarded the plane. Then he'd been sad and tearful, afraid his friend wouldn't talk to him because he was going to be so late home. His mother had managed to get a message through and the friend sent Jacob a text on *his* mother's phone saying he'd saved some cake to share with Jacob as soon as he got there. The lad hadn't stopped smiling since.

'You know I meant next time I'm rostered on to be your paramedic, you ratbag.' Which should be the next visit he had to make for treatment. Joy knew how much she liked being with Jacob and always tried to put them on the same flight. If she did get Joy's job, she wouldn't get to do those special flights with her favourite patients as often. Something else to consider.

Her application was in and still she wondered

Again, transferring their patient was fast and they were back in the air in no time, this time the thumping sound of rotors filling the cabin, and Maxwell was still oblivious to what was going on.

Nick knew he wouldn't relax until the man was off the chopper and being rolled into ED. Only then would he feel safe to breathe properly. They'd done all they could to keep Maxwell alive. It wasn't always enough, but there were limitations even for doctors. The down side to the job.

'Hey.' A light tap on his shoulder. 'Cheer up. We've done well so far.'

Dang, she read him so easily. And made him feel good when she did, not so alone. 'You're right. We have.'

Had the drama diverted her from thinking about her friend and what today meant? She'd been distracted in bed last night, but had thoughts of her friend's demise returned the moment she was back in her own place? Chances were, they had. Leesa didn't hide from pain, instead she seemed to confront it and work through it. He should take a leaf out of her book and do much the same.

if it was the right thing to do. Did she really want to sit behind a desk for hours on end when she could be in the air caring for someone in pain or who was very unwell? Joy did her share of flights when she wasn't tied up with paperwork, as well as discussions with hospital management and other health units, but nothing like the number the rest of the medical crew members did.

There was a bigger question. Did she want to be Nick's boss? It would get in the way of being close friends, something they were rapidly becoming when they weren't being cautious around one another. Worse, it would mean they couldn't be intimate any more. Not when she had to treat all the staff equally. That was essential for good relations, and even if she and Nick continued their fling, she'd follow through on maintaining a level field with everyone. But it would only take one mistake or a perceived error where it appeared Nick was being favoured and she'd be out on her backside.

The other side of this was that Nick had applied too and could end up being her boss. Same issues arose. Plus, she might feel uncomfortable if he was in charge. So far, he came across as eager to work with people, not wanting to be in charge all the time. But she knew how that could be a farce. Hard to imagine that of Nick though. Talk about complicated.

As Darren took off, she leaned her head back and closed her eyes. So many things to consider since Nick had turned up in Cairns. Since returning home she'd been cruising through life, loving her work, enjoying time on the farm with the family and visiting Gran, spending hours with her friends when they were all free at the same time. Giving Baxter all he needed, not necessarily all he wanted. Life had been pretty good.

It still was. Except she'd been living in a vacuum. Taking each day as it came, not looking for more. Not thinking too seriously about her future and the dreams she'd always had about falling in love and raising kids and owning a piece of land with a lovely family home on it.

All very well to think she had years ahead to achieve those dreams, but look what had happened to Danielle. The babies she'd wanted, the trip to Norway to meet her nieces, the career she was building—gone in an instant. Thankfully Danielle hadn't waited to get started on fulfilling her dreams, or she'd not have achieved anything.

'Get a wiggle on, girlfriend. Make the most of today, not tomorrow.'

Leesa's eyes shot open and she looked around. She'd swear Danielle was right here, sitting opposite, locking her formidable gaze on her.

Instead, Nick asked, 'What's up?'

'Nothing. I was daydreaming.'

'What about?'

'Nothing important.' Not half.

'Really?' He sounded disappointed she wasn't sharing.

Something she understood. 'Really.' Some things weren't for imparting to a man she was still getting to know. She closed her eyes again. Hopefully she'd sleep till they reached Cairns. She was tired. Last night had been awesome. Making love with Nick was beyond amazing. She'd also been upset about Danielle. John had added to that with his despair. Yeah, sleep would be good. She sank deeper into the uncomfortable seat and tried to stop thinking about anything.

'Hey, wake up sleepy head. We've landed.' Nick was already out of his seat, looking eager to get going.

After knuckling her eyes, she straightened up and checked the time. Eighteen hundred had been and gone. 'With a bit of luck, we're done for the day.'

Darren poked his head around the cabin doorway. 'I haven't had any notification of another flight.'

'Nothing on the laptop either,' Nick confirmed.

Relief filled her. It had been stressful dealing with Maxwell's cardiac arrests and those horrendous injuries. She'd head out to the farm and have a shower there. Mum was cooking her favourite pasta for dinner as a cheer-her-up treat. Just the thought of diving into the bowl of seafood and spaghetti made her feel a load better. The sleep might've helped too. 'What are you up to tonight?' she asked Nick as he slung the drug kit over his shoulder.

He shrugged. 'A quiet night in.' No smile was forthcoming. He looked tired. It had been as stressful for him working with Maxwell. Probably more so as the doctor on the job. Nick would've taken it hard if their patient hadn't made it as far as the hospital and into emergency care.

'It's been a long day.'

'It has.' He stood back for her to go down the stairs first, barely looking at her. Now that they'd finished work, he appeared to be taking a step back from her. Like her, he might want to think about where they were headed before he got in too deep. She didn't believe he regretted spending time with her. Nick was too genuine for that. He wouldn't have made love and then turned up at work as though they were merely colleagues if something wasn't bugging him. Like her.

Walking into the hangar, she thought about the warmth of being with her family. Something Nick clearly longed for. She sighed. To hell with all this toing and froing about how she felt. They both deserved to relax over a meal with a beer or wine and easy company.

Turning around, she crossed to the supply room. 'Nick, how about joining me and the family for dinner?' If he turned her down it would be the last time she asked.

Slowly he looked across to her. 'Thanks, but think I'll give it a miss. I'm shattered.'

Fair enough. But studying him, her heart tightened at the despondency she saw. He wasn't being entirely truthful. But he also didn't do the feel sorry for me thing. 'Seafood spaghetti marinara is on the menu.'

'How did you know that's one of my favourite meals?' His smile was strained, but it was a smile.

'Something else we have in common. Mum makes it when she thinks I need cheering up.'

'Today you do because of Danielle.'

'Yes.'

'Have I got time to have a shower and throw on some decent clothes that don't smell of antiseptic?'

That was a yes then. Progress. She'd grab the moment and to heck with everything else. 'Go for it. Don't rush. I'll pop down to the supermarket to grab a couple of things Mum needs.'

'Can you add a bottle of wine to the list and I'll fix you up later?'

She shook her head. 'No. Tonight I've invited you out. Your role is to relax and enjoy yourself.'

Along with my company.

No holding back tonight. Danielle was right. Why wait for life to start? It was already here.

'Hey, Mum. I'm at the supermarket. Have you thought of anything else you need?'

'No, Leesa, just the Pinot Noir and tomato paste.' She laughed. 'Not to go together.'

'I'm bringing Nick, the new doctor, with me. Hope that's all right?' Her parents never made a fuss about her turning up with someone extra for a meal but, since it was Nick, she felt she had to say something so that her mum didn't get all gushy when they arrived. Since her Parkinson's diagnosis she'd been keen for Leesa to settle down with someone special.

Her mother laughed again. 'Not even answering.'

There was a bounce in Leesa's step as she made her way along the supermarket aisles. She added a second bottle of wine to the basket before grabbing a couple of items she needed at home, including biscuits for Baxter.

Nick smelt of pine soap when he slipped into the car beside her. His shorts moulded his tight butt, and the blue and white shirt, with two buttons open at the top, made her mouth salivate. Her fingers tightened on the steering wheel to prevent her from leaning over and rubbing his tanned skin. How did she possibly think she could remain aloof around him? He was stunning.

'I'm glad you persisted about me coming. I feel better already.' Nick glanced her way. 'Your family know I'm on the way?'

'Yep. I think Kevin's bringing a couple of mates too. Dad's got some chores to be done in the morning.'

'Count me in. Beats doing the housework.'

'From what I saw your apartment is immaculate.' Almost OTT in her book. 'You might get to drive a tractor tomorrow. There's early cane to be harvested.'

'Could prove interesting. Probably best I stick to the mundane chores.'

'It's no different to driving any other vehicle as long as you keep an eye out where you're going.'

'Could be a new skill to add to my CV.' He laughed for the first time all day, making her pleased she'd suggested he come with her.

She'd asked him as though it was a date, even if he didn't get that. Last night had been wonderful, today a lot less so, and she wanted to find a balance so they could get along—without watching every single thing they said or did for fear of tripping up. 'Being able to do things on a farm beats living in the middle of a large city.'

'I'm starting to see the benefits.'

'What did you used to do in your spare time?'

'In Brisbane I'd go to the Gold Coast to surf and kayak. I'd done some of that in Adelaide but prefer the Coast. In Sydney it wasn't so easy. It takes so long to get to anywhere when you live close to the Central Business District it's a drag.'

'Why the CBD?'

'I was working at the central ambulance station and the rules were that you had to live within sixty minutes of the station, so you could be called in for emergencies. It's a bit extreme really, as everyone on call stayed over at the station anyway, but the advantage for me was not having to take long, tedious train rides to get to work or home at the end of an arduous shift.'

When he relaxed, he could talk a lot. Showed how often he wasn't at ease with people. 'Central Sydney is fabulous,' Leesa said, 'but I could never live there. I prefer the outdoors being handy so I can get out and about any time I like.'

'You've got the farm for that, and all the beaches up the coastline.' He nodded. 'This is a great place. I could see myself staying here longer than my usual stints.'

'You what?' Had he really admitted that? To her?

'Surprised you, have I?' he asked with a serious look. 'Surprised myself, actually. It would be good to stop moving around.'

'Why do you?'

'Habit?' He hesitated. 'I'm looking for somewhere I feel comfortable.'

'Cairns is doing that?'

'Might be.' His uncertainty spoke volumes.

'Give yourself some time before making a major decision. You haven't been here very long.' He mightn't be either, but hope flared.

'True, but I already prefer the work. Flying all over the place to help people with ongoing issues, not having to sit in peak hour traffic when I'm coping with a touch-and-go case. There're a lot of pluses.'

'True.' What about his private life? Any pluses there?

'It's great being invited to dinner with you and your parents.'

She went with his change of subject. Pushing further might lead to him shutting down completely. 'Baxter will be happy to see you.'

He smacked his forehead lightly. 'How could I forget him? He's a big plus to living here.'

'Still thinking you might get a dog?'

'Yes, but if I do, I seriously have to consider moving into a place with a bit of a yard.'

She couldn't imagine Baxter being in an apartment. He loved bounding around the lawn too much. Indicating to turn left, she said, 'Here we go.'

Nick gave her a quizzical glance. 'You sound like you're uncertain about something.'

What about how her mother was going to act around Nick? 'Think the day's catching up.' Her energy level had fallen again, but not as low as when they'd finished work.

'I'm sure a wine and a bowl of spaghetti will have you bouncing around in no time.'

'Fingers crossed you're right.'

And that Mum keeps quiet about certain topics.

Nick would certainly head for another city if he heard a hint of what her mother hoped for.

'That was superb,' Nick told Jodi, Leesa's mother, as he pushed his plate aside. 'Seriously good.'

'Compliments will get you a third helping any day,' Kevin laughed.

He grinned. 'Except someone beat me to the last spoonful.'

'Only the fast win around here,' Kevin said.

'Relax, boys,' Jodi said. 'There's apple crumble and custard to follow.'

Nick shook his head. 'I can't believe this. Amazing.'

Family dinners had never been a part of his life. Not even when growing up with Grandad, who thought meals were to feed the body and not the mind with dreams of delectable offerings. As for what was doled out in foster care, forget it.

One dollop of something that could've been anything the pigs didn't want, and smelt even worse, did nothing for meal times except make them something that had to be got through as fast as possible. One home had been better, he conceded. Mrs Cole had cooked up decent solid meals that everyone had ate in a hurry, before leaving the table to get back to whatever they'd been doing before the plates were put down.

'Tomorrow it's a barbecue after we've finished in the paddocks,' Kevin told him.

'If you're trying to convince me to stay and help out, I'm in.' It was the least he could do for these kind people. Better than out and out admitting he wanted to spend more time with them.

'Might as well stay the night then,' Jodi said with a little smile. 'We've got extra rooms out the back.'

'I haven't come prepared for work. I'll need to pop home and get some rough clothes and boots.'

'Plenty here,' Leesa told him. 'All sizes.'

'Bathroom supplies available too,' Jodi told him.

With everything he needed on hand, he really couldn't insist on returning to town for the night. 'It's a done deal then.' Sipping his beer, he decided it wasn't such a bad thing either. He could get used to this easy way the Bennetts had about them, though no doubt there'd be nothing relaxed about harvest tomorrow. Standing up, he began clearing the dishes from the table.

Yes, he was comfortable beyond description, and for once he couldn't dredge up any enthusiasm over keeping his distance—especially from Leesa. She'd brought him into her circle without any concerns. Inviting him here tonight had come naturally, despite the tension lying between them throughout the day.

Leesa trusted him. Kapow. Just like that, she trusted him.

Talk about a first. Make that the first time he'd trusted in return so readily. Because, yes, he trusted her not to make a fool of him.

He could be making a fool of himself and she'd prove him wrong, but he couldn't find it within himself to believe so. Didn't mean he was going to leap into a relationship with her. They worked together and he didn't want to leave the job he was enjoying so much, especially if he did get the promotion. Also, he'd once fallen in love only to have it thrown back in his face. It had been the final blow to an already fearful heart. He'd lost enough people who mattered. Losing another would be impossible to cope with.

'Take that crumble through to the dining room,' Jodi told him.

'Yes, ma'am.' Leesa often sounded just like her mother, he realised. No arguing with either of them.

'Don't you "yes, ma'am" me.' She playfully

flicked a tea towel at him. 'Pour my daughter another drink so she'll have to stay the night and not rush back to that empty house she lives in.'

'Trying to get me into trouble?' he grinned. He liked this woman. She pulled no punches, again like Leesa. And the rest of the family. 'Tell me, was it tough growing up here when Leesa and Kevin were young?'

'You'd have to ask Leesa. I will say we had no spare money, the kids didn't have fancy clothes or toys, but they both learned to work hard and be proud of what they achieved.'

Though in very different circumstances, he'd had much the same lessons. 'Sounds ideal.' For them, not him. He headed away with the pudding before he got hit with a load of questions he wasn't ready to answer, kind as Jodi was.

Kevin had moved away to talk on his phone and Leesa's father, Brent, was nowhere in sight.

'Would you like another wine?' He knew he was supposed to pour one without giving her the chance to say no, but he preferred to be more onside with Leesa than her mother if it came down to it.

Leesa looked from her empty glass to him, and nodded. 'Why not?' Her eyes shone with laughter. 'You seem comfortable.'

'You know what? I am. I'm even looking forward to going out in the sugar cane fields and getting down and dirty.'

'You might regret that tomorrow night when you've had too much sun, and muscles you aren't aware of ache like stink.'

'You suggesting I'm a townie?'

'Would you expect any different?' she asked and picked up the glass he'd filled. 'Joining me? Or saving yourself for tractor driving?'

A challenge was not to be ignored. He flipped the cap off another beer. Despite being momentarily alone with Leesa he leaned close to say quietly, 'Depends what you mean by joining you.' He could hand out challenges too.

Her smile was so sexy he nearly spilt his beer. 'You're sleeping in the staff quarters.'

'Who else will be there?' Kevin would have his own room in the house, surely? His mates weren't arriving till first thing in the morning as something had come up to keep them in town.

'I might,' Leesa teased.

'Better than me sneaking inside like a horny teen.' What with the noise Leesa made when she came, the whole house would know what was going on.

'I don't know. It could be fun.'

He shivered. He might be comfortable with this family, but there were limitations to how far he took it. 'I'd be too worried we'd be heard to actually let go.'

Leesa's laughter was loud and naughty, and brought everyone back to the table for dessert.

But later when she slipped in beside him on the narrow bed in the staff quarters, he had no hand-brake on his feelings. Nor did Leesa.

The only downside was when she left him to go back to her room around three o'clock. 'I'm acting like that teenager you mentioned, but I can't bear to see a knowing look in my parents' eyes when my alarm goes off and I'm not there to stop it.'

After she'd gone, he slept the sleep of the dead. That was so abnormal he was stunned when Lee-sa's banging on the door woke him.

'What time is it?' The sun was streaming in the window he'd forgotten to cover with the blind.

'Six. I'm heading away. Mum's got breakfast going and the others are already downing mugs of tea.'

He'd been so deeply asleep he hadn't heard their vehicle arriving? 'Great. Now they'll all call me Townie.' He clambered out of bed.

'Take a fast shower before you head over to the house,' Leesa grinned. 'I'll see you tonight.'

He thought she was grinning because he smelt of their night together, but when the water remained cold he had to wonder if she'd been having him on. He wouldn't put it past her.

'Dang, forgot to turn the hot water cylinder on last night,' Brent said when he joined the men around the table. 'We don't leave it on when no one's using the quarters.'

'I'll see to it before we get started in the fields,' Nick told him. 'I'll need a shower before heading back to town.' He didn't want to pong of sweat when Leesa drove him home, hopefully to his apartment for some more fun. Or she might decide to take him to the house she lived in, which he had yet to see. Apparently, it belonged to her grandmother who wasn't ready to sell it, despite living in a retirement village.

'Right. Let's get this happening.' Brent stood up. 'Nick, time for a driving lesson.'

'After I turn the water on,' he returned, feeling so good. Rinsing his plate, he stowed it in the dishwasher and followed the men outside with a spring in his step. To be doing something different and helping this family felt great. It showed how little he did beyond work.

After Patrick gave him his second chance, once he'd begun studying hard to get the grades that got him into university, he'd rarely looked sideways for other interests. His focus had been on proving he was as capable as Judge Crombie had suggested, and now it seemed he didn't know any other way to be.

Leesa was slowly changing him, and through her, her family seemed to be too. Another thing to be careful about? Could be, though a voice was nagging him to let it go and make the most of the opportunity to live a full life, not one that was devoted totally to medicine. He realised he really didn't know how to do that. Didn't have a clue.

'Climb up, Nick. We're heading to that field by the road.'

So began his experience of harvesting.

'How'd that go?' Leesa asked fourteen hours later when she sat down beside him on her parents' deck, where everyone was relaxing with a cold beer.

'He's not bad for a townie,' Kevin answered for him. 'His rows were straight and the cane wasn't mangled.'

'I really enjoyed myself.' Who knew he'd get so much pleasure out of driving a tractor up and down fields in the sweltering heat for hours on end? 'So much so I've put my hand up to help out again when I'm free.'

The smile Leesa gave him increased the happiness. 'Nothing like a new experience to give you a lift.'

She really did understand him. She mightn't

know how messed up he was, but she certainly understood he wanted more out of life than what he already had.

'I wasn't down in the first place.'

'No, but you were looking for something to distract you from work.'

Thank goodness Baxter nudged his knee just then, or he might've grabbed Leesa into a hug that he wouldn't be able to pull back from. Instead, he rubbed the dog behind his ears. 'Hey, boy, is it your dinner time?'

'He's already had it. But no harm in trying to con you into a second round.' Leesa patted Baxter, but he wasn't moving away from Nick's hand.

'Fair enough.' Nick kept rubbing the dog. 'How was work? Busy?'

'Two short flights, one to take a man home after he was discharged from the cardiac ward, another to pick up a tourist who fell off a cliff up in the Daintree and sustained a fractured pelvis.'

'You go by chopper for that one?'

'Yes. It was only a short hop, but not near a road for an ambulance to do the job.' She drained her beer and stood up. 'I'd better give Mum a hand. She seems more tired than usual.'

'She had a restless night,' Leesa's dad spoke up. 'There've been a few of those lately.' The man looked worried.

'The specialist did say that would happen, Dad.

I think a lot of it's to do with her overthinking about what lies ahead.' Leesa frowned. 'Maybe she should have some counselling.'

'Good luck telling her that. She bit my head off the one time I mentioned it.'

'I'm not surprised.' Leesa sighed. 'Mum's always been strong and now she thinks she's letting the side down by being sick.'

'From what I've seen, she's still strong,' Nick said. 'She hasn't given up on getting out and doing her chores and having fun with the family.'

The shaking in her hands had been a bit stronger this morning, but that would happen as time went by. Sometimes it would be because Jodi had done too much, and would revert back to where it had been when she rested, and sometimes the intensity would remain, a sign of the Parkinson's strengthening.

Leesa squeezed his shoulder. 'Thanks for that. I think we're all watching too hard to find something.'

'You're not wrong,' Brent said.

'I imagine it's impossible not to,' Nick agreed. 'It's probably also what Jodi's doing.' He'd seen that with patients when he'd been training. Giving someone a prognosis that had no cure cranked up their anxiety level and had them on guard for more problems. 'It's only natural.'

Leesa was still standing beside him and her thigh was pressing against his arm. 'It's hard.'

He hugged her waist. 'Just remember, these days the outlook is good. Parkinson's can be controlled for years.'

'I know, but this is Mum.'

The only answer he had was to hug harder.

When Leesa stepped away to head to the kitchen she wiped her cheeks quickly, something he'd not seen before. Her mother was obviously her Achilles heel.

Nick's heart tightened for her and this family. There was nothing he could do but be there for her, and them. Something he really wanted. Which was a commitment in itself. One he fully intended sticking to. It was a huge step.

What's more, nothing was getting in the way of it. None of those warning bells were ringing in his head. Whether this meant he was committed to getting closer to Leesa he wasn't sure, but he'd go with this for now and let everything else unfold slowly.

And when they later reached his apartment block, he turned to Leesa. 'Want to come up for a while?' Strange how hard his heart was beating as he waited for her reply. 'Baxter can come too.' Not exactly following the 'slowly' part of his earlier thoughts, but it was impossible not to want to kiss her after what they'd shared last night.

'You didn't think you'd get away with leaving him in the car, did you?'

'I guess not.'

'I'm not staying the night, Nick. You're exhausted after working all day and need some sleep before turning up at the hangar tomorrow. But…' She gave him an impish grin that sent his blood racing. 'I do have an hour to spare.'

Better than nothing.

CHAPTER SIX

THE NEXT MORNING Leesa woke at five. It was a habit, no alarm necessary, though she always set it when on a shift. Today was a day off and she'd go spend some time with her mum.

Stretching as far as possible, she languished in the after sensations of amazing sex the night before. When she'd decided to leap in and see where she and Nick were headed she'd done it with all she had. He was everything she was looking for and more. But it had been physical, not getting close about their future or what each expected.

She couldn't share herself completely with a man who wasn't prepared to talk about himself. Obviously he had issues about family yet seemed completely at home with hers.

Being impatient wasn't going to get her anywhere, so she picked up her phone and texted him.

Morning. Haven't slept so well in ages.

Two hours later when Nick would've been at work, she still hadn't received a reply. Busy? Or playing cool again? Two could play that game, she decided. All very well getting together and having a hot night, and then going back to quiet mode, but she wasn't taking it any more. Either they cleared the air and at least remained friends—though how she'd walk away from their fling was beyond her—or the other option was to stick to being colleagues. Which might be best anyway if either of them got Joy's job.

Climbing out of bed, she hauled on shorts, t-shirt and running shoes. 'Come on, Baxter. I need to clear my head.'

At midday Nick still hadn't come back to her. The pleasure from the night before had well and truly faded. Now she was miffed and wondering if she was wrong about him, that he was another mistake. No, she couldn't accept that. He was special, through and through. Her head knew it, her heart felt it. And yet now she was feeling less inclined to carry on regardless.

Nick had the power to hurt her. A fling with him was no longer enough. It had to be all or nothing. Yet that was all that was on offer, and she knew she couldn't walk away.

She pressed his number to call him. 'Hey, busy morning?' she asked when he answered.

'Has been a bit.'

So that's how it was. 'Okay, I'll leave you to it then.'

'Feel up to going out for a meal tonight?' he asked.

Stunned, she decided she knew nothing when it came to reading men. This one in particular. 'I'd love to.'

'Great. I'll pick you up about seven, unless things turn upside down here.'

'Sounds good.'

'Got to go. There's an emergency come up.'

Wow. Where did that come from? Now she was totally confused. A date with Nick. The first one they'd been on. So far everything had been about sex. Other than Saturday night at the farm, she reminded herself, when she'd invited him to dinner.

Doing a little dance on the spot she hugged herself. If she wasn't in love with Nick, she was so damned close it was scary. Because there were no guarantees everything would go as she hoped. So, she'd go back to taking it slowly, one day at a time, enjoying what time they had together and see where it led.

Which is what she did over the next couple of weeks. Nick was no more forthcoming about his past when they talked over dinner, always bringing the conversation around to work or her family and the farm. Leesa bit down on the questions she needed answers for, hoping that giving him space would eventually lead him to relaxing completely with her.

At the end of one long and difficult day she told Nick she had to go and see her mother. 'I won't drop around to your place tonight. Mum needs me to pick up some meds for her. I want to spend some time with her too.'

'Fair enough.' He looked fine with that apart from a slight shrug.

'It's what I do, Nick, okay? This is my family.' Her life didn't revolve entirely around Nick. She was independent and didn't need him in her life twenty-four-seven. It might be an old hang up from her marriage, but if she didn't take heed she'd only get more wound up. Being around Nick had her freeing herself of the past, but there was a way to go.

'I get it. Truly,' he added sharply.

From the little he'd said, her family life wasn't what he'd known as normal. But he had to understand it if he wanted more than a fling. 'I need to catch up on a few jobs too,' she said. Grocery shopping and tidying the house before Gran came to visit in the weekend were top of the list.

'Me, too.' Finally, he relaxed a little. 'See you back here in the morning.'

'Will do.'

'Leesa.'

Spinning around, she found Nick right behind her. 'Have I forgotten something?'

He shook his head. 'No. I want to say sorry for the way I reacted. I don't expect you to spend every hour of your time with me. We both have more to our lives than work and our fling.'

She stared at him. Coming from Nick that was quite an admission. 'Yes, we do have other things needing our individual attention that can't be ignored for ever.'

I will never become yours or anyone else's total life. Connor tried to make me do that and it was as though he was taking over my mind, dictating who and what I was.

Nick would never be like that, but she still had to stand up and be counted, for her own confidence if nothing else.

Then something dawned on her. 'If you get Joy's job you won't be moving away.'

'No. Think it's time I got on with getting a dog, too.'

'You are looking at more permanence in your life, aren't you?'

That had to be good for him. Might be for her too, because there was no way she wanted to get involved with a man who couldn't put down roots somewhere. But, most importantly, she believed Nick really needed to create his own place and start to feel he was home.

'A pet's a good start,' she added. She wasn't so sure she wanted to go up against him for Joy's job. The consequences might make for more problems.

'One step at a time?'

She dipped her head in agreement. 'Absolutely. Now I have to run or the pharmacy will be closed before I get there.' She touched his stubbly chin. 'Sleep tight.'

'Might do that with no distraction between my sheets.' He stepped away. 'See you in the morning.'

She couldn't wait. Nick had got to her in ways she'd never have believed. He accepted her as she was, didn't even hint at wanting to change her. When she'd said she had other plans for tonight he did tense up a bit, but then he apologised for his reaction. Yes, he was a great guy and she was falling deeper and deeper for him.

Her skin tightened. Was this truly good? Nothing dishonest or untrue was ever reflected in his character, whether they were working together or sharing a meal and bed. Going with her gut instincts felt right. If those needed back up it was there in the way her family accepted Nick. Not what they'd done with her ex. No, they'd tried to warn her Connor wasn't good enough but love could be blind. It had been with Connor. It wasn't going to be with Nick.

Next morning when she walked into the staff kitchen her heart melted at the sight of Dr Sexy perched on a stool, stirring sugar into his tea as he read what appeared to be case notes. 'Morning.'

His head flicked up. 'Back at you. Kettle's just boiled.'

'Who's flying us today?'

'Darren. He's giving the plane the once over.'

Mark, a helicopter pilot, strode into the room. 'I'm on the chopper if you need an exciting ride.'

'Not unless an emergency crops up,' Nick told him with a laugh. 'Our list is all about going to places with landing strips, not pocket-sized squares.'

'What time did you get in?' Leesa asked.

'Just after five. I was out of milk and bread so figured I might as well grab some and come in here for breakfast.'

Sounded like he hadn't slept well. Missing the fun they'd been getting up to?

'Thought you were going shopping last night.' She wasn't going to tell him she'd slept like a log. He might think she didn't miss him much, and she had.

She'd also been glad of time to herself to think through everything going on between them. The past fortnight had sped past, all fun and not serious in any way. Which was fine, but nothing had changed. All fun and no depth.

'I went home to shower and change, then couldn't be bothered going out again.'

'Where are we headed for our first job?' she asked, ready to get to work and away from wondering if Nick ever relaxed enough to get out and have a life. He'd helped at the farm but that had been at her instigation. It was as though he didn't know what to do with himself when he wasn't being a doctor.

'Taking a woman down to Brisbane for a heart valve replacement. She's expected here at eight thirty.'

'I'll go check stock levels and everything else.' With a mug of tea in hand, Leesa headed out to the plane, all the time trying not to think about Nick. Impossible when they spent a lot of time together.

'How was Jodi?' Nick asked as they waited on board for their patient to arrive.

'Not as tired as I'd expected. I do wish she'd take things easier though.'

'You might be asking too much.'

She knew that, but she didn't want her mum's condition getting worse before it had to. 'Of course I am. It's to be expected.'

'I get that.'

Did he though? When he'd said he didn't have family to care about? She sucked air over her teeth. Now she was being bitchy for no reason.

It was because he rattled her. They were opposites in so many ways but they still understood each other. Could they have a future? One that was for ever and not just for a few nights having amazing sex?

'You've gone quiet.'

'It happens occasionally,' she put out there.

'Can't say I've noticed.' Nick tapped her shoulder. 'We've got company.'

The ambulance was backing up to the plane. 'Good. Now we can get going.'

'Impatient, aren't we?' He flicked her a puzzled look.

'It's a long haul to Brisbane and back.'

'Part of the job.' The puzzlement remained.

Fair enough. She didn't know why she was being terse other than she needed more time away from Nick to do some serious thinking. She was in a relationship that she wasn't sure was quite what she wanted, or needed. A fling had its upsides, but they weren't really her thing. She was an all or nothing kind of girl. And that didn't seem to be what Nick wanted.

'Hello, Leesa, Nick. This is Maggie Oldsmith.' The ambulance medic was pressing the button to bring the stretcher up to their level. 'She's been given a mild sedative as she's not keen on flying.'

'Hi, Maggie. I'm Leesa, your paramedic for the duration of the trip.'

'And I'm Nick, the doctor keeping an eye on you.'

'Hello. I'm the old bat needing a new heart valve.' Maggie's smile was tired, as were her eyes. It all went with her heart condition.

'You'll be a new woman when we bring you home,' Leesa told her.

'I hope so.'

'Is there anyone coming with us to keep Maggie company in Brisbane?' Nick asked the medic as he looked outside.

'Maggie's son is already down in Brisbane. He'll be at the hospital when the ambulance arrives.'

'Right, let's get this show in the air.' Nick checked the trolley was secure. Leesa watched the medic lower the lift and move away so she could close the door.

'All set,' she told Darren.

Once they were airborne and levelled out, Nick gave Maggie a thorough check over, leaving Leesa redundant as the two of them chattered about any number of things.

She knew Nick was trying to divert Maggie from worrying about flying. It must've worked, or the sedative had had an effect, because she was soon snoring. The monitors were showing no changes in her readings from what they'd been at the start of the flight. 'Well done.'

'Not sure I like the background music,' he

grinned, then pulled up the laptop and began going through Maggie's medical data, the grin gone.

So no chatting to fill in the time. Leesa sighed. They did do this at times, pulled back from one another without reason. It was quite likely Nick required space to think it all through too. That was a wet blanket on her emotions even when she was doing the same. Talk about mixed up, she smiled internally. But then the experts said love wasn't meant to be easy. She wouldn't know other than her experience definitely hadn't been a walk in the park.

Staring out the window she watched the coastline bend and curve all the way south. It was a beautiful landscape. The beaches, the blue water and the Great Barrier Reef further out attracted visitors from all over the country and around the world. She lived in one of the most amazing places.

Time to check on Maggie. She unclipped her seatbelt at the same moment Nick did.

'I've got this,' he said.

She could get picky and point out she usually did the obs, but what was the point? They were as capable as each other and Maggie was in good hands, be they hers or Nick's.

'No problem.' Pulling her phone from her pocket, she read her emails and answered two.

* * *

On the return flight Nick studied Leesa from under lowered brows. Damn she ripped him up and had his heart speeding without any encouragement. She was beyond wonderful. The nights they spent in bed were amazing. He couldn't get enough of her. So much so he was teetering on the edge of the love cliff. More than anything he wanted to let go and hand his heart over. Yet the buts remained, holding him firmly on the ground. He knew his love would be safe with Leesa if she reciprocated it.

That was the question. Did she? There was so much he hadn't told her, and the longer he left it the harder it became to put everything out there. As though the more he gained from being with her, the more he had to lose when she learned about his past and how he'd raced into his marriage without so much as a backward glance.

He gave a tight grunt. Seemed these days the only way he looked was backwards. Keeping safe. Staying lonely and fed up. Desperate for something most people had. Afraid of being hurt and of hurting someone else.

'Cleared to land,' Darren told them.

'Good, I'm starving.' Leesa slid her phone into her pocket.

'When aren't you?' Nick asked. He wasn't

only referring to food, but sex. Leesa had a huge appetite for that.

They'd barely started lunch when an emergency call came in. It had them heading to Cook Town, to pick up a fisherman who'd got his hand caught in the winch while bringing in a laden net, and had severed two fingers.

'How awful was that?' Leesa commented after they'd loaded the man into an ambulance back in Cairns. She shuddered at the thought of losing some fingers.

'I bet it won't stop him fishing once the stubs have healed,' Nick said. 'He sounded like a tough bugger. Apparently, he once had a large fish hook stuck in his abdomen for two days while the skipper got the boat back to port in the midst of a storm.'

'How did the hook end up in his stomach?' she asked. 'Kevin's told me some crazy stories about what happens on board fishing trawlers.'

'It's not the safest job about.'

Joy was waiting outside the hangar when they arrived back at base. 'You two are needed on the chopper. A six-seater fixed-wing with four people on board has gone down in the forest behind Hartley's Falls. Fire and emergency have one chopper on its way and need another. You're the first crew I've got available.'

'Let's go.' Leesa was already striding towards the chopper where Mark was sitting in the cockpit.

Nick strode out to keep. 'No rest for the wicked, eh?'

'I'm wicked?' she teased.

'Very,' he grinned. The tension had eased.

'Takes one to know one,' she added as she leapt up into the helicopter.

Nick slammed the door closed behind them.

Mark instantly started the rotors spinning. 'Buckle up, guys. I'm going low and fast.'

Which meant they could get knocked about by wind off the hills. But it was totally reasonable to do that. They weren't going too far and Mark wouldn't want to waste time gaining height that he'd soon have to lose.

'What do we know about the passengers?' Nick asked when they were airborne.

'Four men returning from a safari up north,' Mark answered, 'One of them the pilot. The plane lost contact with the tower about an hour ago. A chopper from Port Douglas was in the vicinity and located the plane. There's no movement, no sign of anyone.'

'We're to expect the worst-case scenario and hope we're wrong.' Nick leaned back in his seat, his eyes closed. 'I hate these jobs.'

'Don't we all?' Leesa agreed.

Nick sat up straight. 'Let's run through what we need to take down when we arrive.'

Leesa tapped one finger. 'The medical packs.' Tapped a second finger. 'The drug kit.'

He nodded. 'Stretchers, oxygen.'

They continued with the list, both working on the assumption they'd be retrieving men who were alive. It was the only way to approach the scene, unless they heard differently.

The closer they got to Hartley's Falls the tighter the tension in Leesa's face got. They hadn't heard from the other chopper yet.

Nick touched her thigh. 'Breathe.'

'I'm trying,' she gasped.

'I get that.' He kept rubbing her thigh.

Mark came through the headset. 'All four men are alive. Three with serious injuries. Fire and Rescue are lifting two out soon, the medics have stabilised them and got them onto stretchers.'

'We're going to have to hover further away?' Nick asked.

'If I can't find a safe place to put down nearby, then yes.'

'What if you got the other chopper to move away so we can be lowered to the site to help out?'

'We'll do it only if the guys on the ground give us the all-clear, but chances are they'll be too busy retrieving their two patients.'

'We don't want to delay their operation.'

A low groan came through the headset.

'Mark, what's up?' Leesa asked.

Silence.

'Mark? Talk to us,' Nick demanded.

'Buckle up tight,' Mark shouted. 'I'm going down.' Even before Mark finished speaking the chopper was dropping. Fast. Frighteningly fast.

His heart in his throat, Nick glanced at Leesa as she pulled her seatbelt tighter. 'What's going on?' His stomach was a tight ball. Something was very wrong. 'Hey, Mark, what's up?'

'Don't feel good.'

'How? Where?'

'Head.'

'Not good.' Leesa stared ahead.

Nick reached for her shaking hand, held it between both his. 'We'll be fine.' They had to be. Leesa had to be. Nothing bad could happen to her.

Leesa would've given Nick an eye roll if fear wasn't gripping her so hard no part of her moved—except her mind, and it was in panic mode.

'Yeah, sure.' Her fingers tightened around his, probably about to break them. What was wrong with Mark? Something to do with his head. Pain? Blurriness? She glanced out the window, and immediately looked away.

The forest was barely metres below, rushing at

them. Then trees were all around and the chopper was tipping sideways. A horrendous racket filled her head of tearing metal, rotors ripping into the trees. *Bang! Ka-thump!* Metal screeched, buckled inwards. She was flung sideways, then backwards.

The movement stopped.

Nick's hand had gone.

She blinked once, twice. Stared around, breathed in deep. 'Nick?' she cried. 'Nick. Answer me.'

'I'm here.' His voice came from beyond where he'd been sitting. 'You okay?'

No idea. She tried to stretch her legs but didn't get far because the cockpit had been shoved back. The stretcher in front of her was at an odd angle. Her upper right arm was throbbing. Her neck was stiff and painful. Otherwise, 'Think so. What about you?'

His reply was a deep groan as he tried to shift.

Her heart jerked. 'Nick? What's happened?' *Please be all right.* Unclipping the safety harness, she stood up only to bang her head on metal. The top of the chopper was caved in. Down on her knees, she forced her way over obstacles to reach Nick.

His face was contorted with pain.

Her heart slowed. 'Where are you hurting?' Nothing could be wrong with Nick. Anything but that.

'My chest. Probably my ribs. Check Mark. I'll follow you.'

'No.' She wanted to stay with Nick, check him over thoroughly. Laying her hand on his chest she touched his ribs as gently as possible.

He winced. 'Something slammed into my chest, possibly cracked a rib or two. I don't feel bad otherwise. Mark was having a medical event. He needs your attention.'

Nick was right. Dammit.

'You stay here.' She was already backing out of the small space beside him. It was the hardest thing she'd ever done. Her arms ached with the need to hold him, to confirm what she knew. They were alive.

Leesa grabbed a seat as the chopper lurched and dropped further to thud onto something solid, hopefully the ground. The thought of falling further gave her the heebies.

'Agh…' Nick groaned loudly.

'Nick?' she called, her heart in her throat as she prepared to go back to him.

'Carry on to Mark. He didn't respond to your call.' Then Nick groaned again, followed by a curse.

'Mark, can you hear me?' She pushed and shoved through the crumpled wreck of the helicopter. 'Mark? Where are you?'

Silence. But only from him. Trees were cracking and metal was groaning as the chopper rocked. She closed her eyes and waited for it to fall further.

Nothing happened.

Slowly she exhaled. Phew. A pounding started behind her eyes. She couldn't feel a wound on her skull, didn't remember hitting anything with her head.

Get over it.

Squeezing through the unrecognisable flying machine, nothing appeared to be where it should. A pair of legs stopped her progress.

'Mark.' Leesa knelt and began to run her hands up Mark's legs to his arms and hopefully a pulse. A branch had bust through the windscreen making it impossible to see his head. Her hand touched a hand, and she felt for a pulse. Very weak but there *was* one. Relief filled her. Not that it meant he was going to be all right, but he was alive. Holding the back of her other hand in front of his mouth and nose she felt erratic, short breaths. 'What happened?' she asked no one in particular.

He'd said 'head' when Nick asked where the problem was. Could be an aneurism or a stroke. Impossible to tell.

Unwilling to try moving Mark on her own when she didn't know what other injuries he might have, she began to carefully and methodically check over the parts of his body she could reach.

'What have we got?' Nick asked from behind her.

She nearly leapt out of her skin. 'Jeez, you scared the living daylights out of me. You were supposed to stay where you were.' She wasn't going to admit she was glad he was with her. This whole disaster was freaking her out. Her hands shook and the throbbing behind her eyes was increasing in intensity.

A steady hand touched her shoulder. 'It was getting a bit lonely back there.'

Looking at him, she bit her lip. He was whiter than white. 'It's a tight squeeze in here but I'm glad you're with me.' So much for not telling him. 'You're bleeding from your chin.' She ran a finger over his jaw.

'Took a bit of a whack. Is Mark alive?' Forthright for sure. But sensible—there was no point in trying to move the man if he was gone.

'He's breathing and his pulse is shallow and hard to find. I haven't managed to check him all over. That branch's in the way. Before you even think of trying to move it with those ribs giving you grief, you are staying away.'

Talking like a kid on steroids, Leesa.

'Sorry, I'm a bit shaken up.'

Nick ran a finger down her cheek. 'It's understandable. I'm feeling much the same.'

She leaned closer, drew a slow breath to ease the tension gripping her. It was so good having him here, if only he hadn't been injured. 'Take it easy. You're hurting.'

'I hear you, but let me take a look at Mark. There might be some way we can shift him without causing any more problems. We need to make certain his spine's not damaged first.' Nick was already removing one of Mark's shoes. A hard pinch on the sole got a small twitch. 'Don't think we need worry about the spine at least.'

'Something on his side.' Seemed all she could do was hope for more good news to come.

Worry belied Leesa's words and Nick wanted to haul her into his arms and never let go. The crash had been close to being dreadful for all of them. Holding Leesa would calm his shattered nerves, but Mark needed his attention more than anyone. Scrambling closer, he bit down hard as pain flared in his chest. The odds of fractured ribs were high. He was thankful his breathing was fine or he'd be scared witless that a rib had penetrated a lung.

'I wonder how long before someone realises we're missing.' Leesa had a hand on Mark's wrist, her finger searching for his pulse. She must've found it because relief filtered through her worry.

'They must've heard from Mark that we were closing in.' Quite the day for aircraft crashes. 'Someone will be asking why he hasn't reported in shortly.' The pilot's left arm was at an odd angle. 'Possible shoulder dislocation here.' Nothing he could do about it. Mark needed to be in an open space for the joint to be manipulated into place, and until help arrived that wasn't happening. Not a lot was.

'Can you reach his head to check it over?' Leesa sounded stronger.

Relieved, Nick held his breath as he lay down prone next to Mark, reaching his right arm up to Mark's head. Pain engulfed him. He waited for it to pass, trying not to breathe too deeply, then took his time feeling for contusions. 'Nothing.' But… 'Hang on. Yep, swelling on the left side.' A bleed? Quite possible, though prior to the crash or as a result of that branch whacking was impossible to know yet.

'Should we try to put him into the recovery position?' There was a hitch in Leesa's voice. 'Just in case.'

In case things went pear-shaped. 'Let's give it a go.' It was going to hurt like stink but they had to do everything they could for Mark. 'You'll have to do most of the work, I'm sorry.' His left side was pretty useless.

'I'll try pulling him my way if you want to work at keeping him free of the branch.'

It was an operation in hell, painful for all of them, though Mark knew nothing. Eventually they had him on his side with his head tipped back enough to keep his mouth open.

Nick took a couple of deep breaths and pushed up onto his backside. 'You cried out a couple of times. Are you sure you're not injured somewhere?'

His heart pounded at the thought. He didn't want Leesa hurting at all. The chances of that were nigh on impossible. The severe landing and then the chopper rolling and twisting meant there was no escaping some serious bruising for all of them. They were lucky both of them weren't far worse off. That's if she wasn't downplaying an injury—something that wouldn't surprise him. Leesa was one determined woman when it came to showing how strong she could be.

Her eyes met his. 'I honestly don't think I've got anything more than lots of bruises. We're going to look a funny colour for a few days.'

'A matching pair.' Crash survivors. What if he'd lost her for ever? Strong shivers rocked him. No way. He couldn't face that. She was special, wonderful. She—

His heart stopped. Leesa meant so much to him it was terrifying thinking about what might've happened.

Leesa's delicious lips finally lifted into one of her beautiful, gut-twisting smiles. 'Does purple match the blue of our uniforms?'

He shuffled closer, needing to put his good arm around her. He had to feel her, to know they'd made it. Kissing the top of her head, he whispered, 'We're very lucky.'

'We are. For a moment…'

His arm tightened around her as she shivered. 'Don't go there.' He already had. It was dark and gut wrenching.

'I'll try not to.' Her lips brushed his. 'Hold me close.'

He twisted to bring her in closer, and gasped as pain shot through his chest.

Leesa pulled back carefully. 'Nick. I'm so sorry. I didn't think. Where's it hurting?' Her fingers were slipping under his shirt, going right to the very spot where he thought the ribs were broken.

'How did you know?'

'That that's where it's painful? There's a lot of swelling. Plus, some bleeding from a surface wound.' Her fingers were moving all over his ribcage, checking, feeling, touching. Then she moved lower to check his abdomen, up to his shoulders and around his neck. 'Otherwise, I think you're up to muster. Unless,' her eyes were fierce when she locked them on him. 'Unless there's something *you're* not mentioning?'

He started to laugh and immediately regretted it as his ribs told him they weren't in the mood. On a light inhale he croaked out, 'I'm fairly certain all's good inside.'

'Thank goodness.'

Another gentle kiss came his way, soft on his mouth, yet tormenting—he couldn't follow up by embracing her hard and kissing her like there was no tomorrow, because there nearly hadn't been.

But they did have a tomorrow. They'd survived the crash, were able to move and talk and be together. For now. He pressed his mouth over Leesa's, savouring the moment, her warmth and softness. Who knew when they'd get a chance to do this again? A crowd would soon arrive to help. Far more important, he knew, but he did need to hold Leesa, if only to confirm she had survived.

She pulled back and stared around. 'Where is everyone? Come on, guys. We need you.' Her gaze returned to him. 'I presume the locator beacon still works after a crash like this.'

'They're made to withstand huge impact. The rescue crews already had their hands full, and they're now one chopper down. Literally,' he added quietly.

'I wonder if Kevin's with a crew. He's a volunteer for Port Douglas's Fire and Rescue and wasn't out on the boat today.'

'Do they bring that station in on these events?'

'Yes. We're closer to Port Douglas than Cairns.' Leesa tipped her head to one side. 'Listen. Is that what I think?'

A low *thwup* sound reached him, getting louder by the second. 'Only a chopper makes that racket.' Hopefully those on board were looking for them. 'That hasn't taken too long.'

'They'll do a recce to see what's happened and then assess how badly injured we are.'

The helicopter seemed to be doing a circle above them, creating a sharp wind and causing small objects to flip around the wreckage. Then it moved away a small distance and hovered briefly before retreating further. 'We might be getting some company.'

Leesa had leaned over Mark to shield him from the dust filling the air. 'Hope so.'

'Hey, Mark, you there?' a familiar voice called. 'Leesa, Nick?'

'We're here. Everyone's alive,' Nick called back as Kevin appeared through the trees. 'Leesa's bruised but otherwise seems in good nick.' The guy would've been worried sick once he heard his sister was on board the chopper. 'Mark needs evacuating ASAP.'

'Kevin, am I glad to see you.' The relief in Leesa's face nearly undid Nick.

He knew she'd been holding it together, but now that help had arrived in the form of her brother, she was obviously letting go a little. He wasn't someone she'd feel she had to keep her game face on for. Which she'd been doing with him, he realised. That hurt. Yet it was who she was, and that was the woman he was falling for more and more. He gripped her hand. 'You're doing well, Leesa.'

She blinked at him, then dredged up a smile. 'Sorry, just had a wee lapse of concentration.' Turning back to Kevin, she said, 'Have Mum and Dad heard about this?'

'What do you think, Leesa? It's not a large town when it comes to these scenarios.'

'True.'

Kevin hugged her carefully, obviously not taking his word about her condition for granted. 'Hell, girl, you know how to frighten us all.' Pulling back, he swallowed hard. 'Nick, how are you faring? Any injuries?'

'Think I've got a broken rib or three, otherwise all good. It's Mark who's the worry.'

'Fill me in on the help required.'

Leesa nodded to him. 'You're the doc.'

Kevin listened while sussing out how to get Mark out of the wreckage. 'Got it. I need Tony down here to give me a hand.' He talked into his handset, then told them, 'We'll take Mark to hospital now, but I'm afraid you two will have to wait a while. The two people at the original accident site you were going to need attention.'

'No problem,' Leesa and Nick said at the same time.

Nick managed a smile. They were in sync and it felt good.

'Though there is a seat for one of you on this trip, but I don't like the idea of leaving either of you on your own.'

'Take Leesa.'

'No way. I'm staying,' she snapped. 'We'll be fine. Get Mark sorted. He's in a bad way.'

'On to it. Leesa, I'll let Ma and Pa know you're okay.'

'Tell them Nick's all right too.'

An unfamiliar tenderness struck him in his chest. Leesa included him in what to tell her family like it was nothing unusual. Given how open and friendly they all were to him, he wasn't really surprised. They had no idea how foreign that was for him.

Spending time with Leesa's family didn't make them his. They had treated him how he imagined they treated most people—with open hearts and kindness. All the more reason to step back before he got too involved and hurt Leesa by messing it up somehow. Because he wasn't great at family relationships, if his history was anything to go by.

It was awfully quiet after the helicopter had left with Mark. Nick held Leesa against his good side and laid his chin on top of her head. 'You doing okay?'

'I've had better days.'

She wasn't opening up to him, but that could be her coping mechanism. She hadn't said much to Kevin either after that first comment.

'Haven't we all? I hope Mark's going to come out of this all right. It's amazing how he did his best to get us on the ground while he still could.'

'We owe him our lives.'

A shiver went through him. They certainly did.

Leesa held his hand tight against her thigh, her fingers shaking. 'I—' Tears streaked down her face.

His heart thumped against his ribs, creating even more pain. He needed to take her in his arms and never let go again. What if? It was a question he knew he'd be asking himself for a long time to come. Reaching for her, he held her carefully, knowing he *would* have to let her go eventually. He'd nearly lost her. As he had lost others he'd loved. It was too much.

He wasn't meant to love. He was meant to run solo. Yet how could he leave her?

CHAPTER SEVEN

IT WAS CRAMPED and beyond uncomfortable sitting in the wreckage. Leesa slowly turned in his embrace, being careful of Nick's ribs, and gazed at him before finding a weak smile. 'Still enjoying your job?'

'I'm getting new experiences every day.'

'Glad to hear it. I'd hate for you to think you'd prefer to be on the ambulances instead the planes.' Though that would be a lot safer. Unless some crazed driver drove into the ambulance.

Doing glum again, Leesa. You're alive and so is Nick.

'What made you choose ambulance work over other options when you qualified?' Time to see if she could learn more about this mysterious man. She was done with messing around, deciding what she wanted to do. Today had woken her up. She adored Nick.

'I like the intensity of picking up people from all sorts of places and traumas and working to save them. I have to be at my best all the time.'

'Doesn't any doctor worth their weight?'

'True, but there's often an urgency that doesn't come with sitting in an office talking about symptoms and past medical history. I like being out and about rather than tied into one place all the time.'

'I know what you mean. It's why I swapped from nursing to the ambulances.'

Was that really why he did this kind of emergency medicine? It sounded a bit like how he moved from city to city to town every year or two. He didn't seem to do getting close to people. They were already involved, though for how long she had no idea.

Last night she'd been thinking about slowing down and taking a long hard look at what she was doing. Today she'd come close to not having that choice—and she wanted him. Badly. To prove she had survived. That Nick had survived. To prove she did have a future. Hopefully with Nick. She wasn't going to waste any more time procrastinating. If the crash had shown her anything, it was to get on and make the most of what came her way.

Turning the conversation onto him, she said, 'Tell me more about why you keep moving around the country.'

He tensed.

She waited for him to change the subject. Or not speak at all.

Finally, 'I don't know what it's like to stop in one place. To live in the same town, or home even, permanently.'

Her heart plummeted. She couldn't imagine what that was like. 'Not even when you were growing up?'

'No.' His fingers were rubbing soft circles on her arm. 'My parents died about the time I turned one. My grandfather took me in but he passed when I was twelve.'

'Nick, that's terrible.' Taking his hand in both hers she held tight.

'It sucks all right.'

'No one deserves that. I don't know how you coped.' She'd always had her family beside her. A loving, caring family who looked out for each other no matter what. Even when she went ahead and had married Connor. They'd believed he was wrong for her, but they'd never left her to deal with the aftermath on her own.

'Who says I did?'

'I do. Look at you. A doctor helping others. A kind man who doesn't put himself before everyone else. You work hard, and—' She found a smile for him. 'You love dogs. Baxter anyway.'

Nick stared at her as if she'd gone mad.

'I didn't hit my head in the crash.' At least she didn't think she had. 'I mean every word.'

One corner of his mouth lifted. He flattened his lips but the smile returned, this time with his whole mouth involved. 'No wonder I moved up here. You say the most wonderful things.'

Her heart clapped. Damn he was wonderful. Even when she wasn't looking for a future with him, he was so tempting. Dr Sexy. 'Glad to make you happy.'

'Remind me to buy Baxter a bone next time I see him too. Seems I've made another friend.'

'You've made a few. Everyone at Flying Health Care thinks you're great. As for my family, Mum's always asking when you're next coming to dinner.' She winced. That info should've stayed in her head.

There'd been a few times where Mum had quizzed her about Nick to the point she looked for excuses not to phone. A girl had to look out for herself, sometimes even from interfering mothers.

'You need to buy a whole bag of bones,' she added. Might as well go for light-hearted and keep him onside. It would be mighty lonely in here if he decided to clam up on her.

'I'll do that.'

'Where did you live with your grandfather?'

'Adelaide. Although he was tough, Grandad

was good to me, gave me the basics in life. In some ways he was my father, my only parent, because I don't remember anything about my mum and dad.' Then he'd lost the man replacing his parents.

'Of course you don't remember. Have you got photos of your parents?'

'A box full. But the weird thing is they've never grown up. They were only twenty and twenty-one when they died. I know that probably doesn't make sense, but I can't help it.'

'It makes perfect sense to me. I can see you as a boy looking at those photos and hoping for something to change. You're now older than they were, and that must seem strange.'

'Leesa, you're so understanding it's scary.' He leaned in to kiss her, wincing as he moved. Guess the shock of the crash was causing havoc with the sensible side of his brain.

'Careful, Nick. You can't take that pain for too long. How about I get you a strong opioid? You've got to get through moving out of here and onto a chopper yet.'

'Might be a good idea, though I'm not supposed to prescribe them to myself.'

'I'm qualified to give drugs out, remember?'

'Glad one of us has their wits about them. My doctor head is getting in the way. I'll put that down to the unusual circumstances I find myself in.'

She wasn't so sure she had any wits, but she could pretend. 'I'll find the kit.'

On her hands and knees, she crawled through the wreckage to search for the drug kit. Equipment lay everywhere, bags and packs broken open. One monitor was smashed, the other looked as though nothing was wrong with it. Unbelievable.

Scrabbling around she finally found what she needed. Hopefully everything inside was in good shape, or Nick might miss out on dealing with that pain. He couldn't swallow a handful of powder if he didn't know what it was.

Swallow. Water. Looking around again she spied a pack of six bottles they carried for patients and staff. Two remained whole. Damn, it was almost pitch dark now. Torch. Where were they kept? Top shelf of the cupboard by the bed. She squinted through the dark to see where the cupboard was. There, twisted on the floor. The door was warped. She pulled to open it but it wouldn't budge. Swearing gave her some satisfaction, but did not help get the door to move.

'Damn. No torches.' She needed to get back to Nick while she could still see enough to read the labels on the bottles of tablets.

Back beside Nick, she went through the bottles of drugs. 'Which one do you want?'

'Codeine.'

Holding a bottle right before her eyes, she laughed, although a bit sharply. 'Good choice. Here it is. At least I think that's what it says.' She handed it to Nick. 'What do you see?'

'Codeine.' He handed it back.

Tipping one tablet into the palm of his hand, she opened a water bottle and pushed it into his other.

Nick's head reared. A tight groan ripped out of his mouth.

'Did I hurt you? I'm so sorry.' Her heart was thudding. She'd hurt him. How could she be so thoughtless? Guilt assailed her. 'Nick, I didn't mean to.'

He placed his palm on her cheek. 'It's all right. You didn't do anything wrong. I moved sharply and paid the price.'

Her heart skittered. It hurt her to see him in pain. 'We might have to ban kissing for a few days,' she said.

That would be bloody hard to stick to. Kissing Nick was her favourite pastime these days. As much as making love. Sometimes a kiss from Nick made her feel right, happy and content, and she didn't need the excitement of sex to do that.

'Not if I have a say in the matter.' He sagged

back against the metal upright that had avoided being bent in the hard landing. 'But I will give things a rest for now. We might have a longish wait before help arrives. It's going to take a while to airlift the others to hospital.'

Time alone with Nick. She'd love it, except he was in pain. 'I reckon everyone's working their butts off to get here ASAP.'

They'd better be. She surreptitiously watched Nick's chest rise and fall with each breath he took. Consistent, not deep, but not too shallow, nor out of kilter. Good. If his lung had been punctured by one of those fractured ribs he'd be in a much more serious condition.

'Because we're part of the team?' He nodded. 'Makes sense I suppose. I've seen police go that extra mile for their own when something terrible has happened.'

'It's a natural response. Look after your own first.'

They sat squashed in the confined space as darkness took over completely. Now that she was sitting still with nothing to do, aches all over her body were starting to get ferocious.

'I got lucky as a teen when I stole a car.'

'You what?' She'd never have believed it if she'd heard it from anyone else, but Nick didn't do lying.

'I wanted to learn to drive and no one would

teach me. The judge gave me a second chance and I grabbed it with both hands, never did anything so stupid again.'

Now she was learning what made him tick. 'Tell me more.'

'His son was in my class and cruised through every lesson like he didn't need to put in any effort. I made him my target, to beat him in all subjects.'

That she believed. 'And did you?'

'Not all, about fifty-fifty. It meant he had to knuckle down and work hard for the first time. Patrick—Judge Crombie—credits me for Darian's success, says he'd never have done so well if I hadn't caused him a headache.'

'Patrick. So you're still in touch?'

'He's been my mentor ever since, though we don't catch up often. I flew down to Adelaide to see him before I came up here. He had cancer but is in remission. Who knows for how long? He's been warned to get on with ticking things off his bucket list.'

Leesa grabbed his hand. 'That's hard for you too. But you did get lucky with him.'

'I did.' He removed his hand. 'Tell me about your husband.'

Blindsided by the sudden change, she took a moment to collect her thoughts. This was part of moving forward into a stronger relationship, and yet she felt he was suddenly aware of how much he'd given away about himself and regretted it.

'Connor was amazing,' Leesa began. 'So kind and generous, helpful, keen to be a part of my life. I fell for him fast and we married, against my family's wishes I admit, and we moved to Brisbane for his career. End of the happy days. It was as though he was free to do what he liked being so far from my family. He was clever, changing slowly, not showing his true colours straight up. I wasn't good enough for him. Didn't matter what it was, cooking his favourite meal, parking the car in the garage, mowing the lawns, I couldn't do anything right, and I paid by being snubbed, then access to our bank accounts was closed off to me.'

Leesa shivered. He'd never hit her, but there were days when she half expected it.

'But you left him.'

'I did.' She could hear the pride in her voice. 'I had to or submit for ever, and I wouldn't do that. It wasn't easy, but I did it and stayed on in Brisbane to prove to myself I didn't need to run home.'

'Except you then faced another bully.'

'By then I'd wised up. He didn't stand a chance. Not with me, and he backed off. The other women didn't do so well until I supported them. After dealing with my husband, I knew how hard it

can be for some people to leave these situations.
I couldn't stand by and not help them.'

With one finger on her chin, Nick turned her
face so he was looking directly at her with empa-
thy. 'I imagine trust doesn't come easy for you.'

Like she thought, smart. 'You got it.' She was
working on getting over her issues about her ex,
but it wasn't as easy as packing up and leaving
him had been, and that hadn't been a picnic either, with him refusing to accept that she was
never going back. He kept telling her she'd never
manage on her own, which only reminded her
how she'd coped at school and could do it again,
even if it was trickier.

'How's your trust radar after your marriage
fell apart?' she asked.

His sigh was long and slow. 'Not great. Makes
me wonder if I'm cut out for a relationship, or if
I should remain single and get on with being a
good doctor instead.'

'Don't think like that. One mistake doesn't
make a lifetime's worth.' Said she who'd thought
the same for so long.

Not any longer. Danielle had always said she
had to move on, and after today that's exactly
what she intended doing. With Nick. And if that
didn't work out? She'd keep trying. Her chest
ached. As a result of the impact, or because she
wanted a man to love and kids to raise under

that love, she couldn't be certain. Probably both. She shuffled her butt, trying to get comfortable, not doing well. Tipping her head back she closed her eyes, exhaustion filling her, closing down her mind.

'Chopper's coming,' Nick nudged her.

She hadn't heard it but now it was very obvious. 'Phew. I've had enough of this place.'

'No food or anything to drink,' Nick smiled. 'The TV screen was useless too.'

'Funny man. Now we can get you checked over and make sure those ribs haven't done any damage to your lung.'

'My breathing's normal.'

'Yeah, I have been keeping an eye on your chest movements,' she admitted. Not hard when his chest was so damned distracting. She still worried he was hiding another injury from her.

'No surprise there.'

Tenderness filled Nick as Leesa gave him a wobbly smile. As though now they were about to be lifted out of here, she was letting go of whatever had kept her calm till this moment.

He wanted to kiss her once more before they were surrounded by their rescuers. It hurt to lean closer but, hell, he could deal with that to taste Leesa under his lips.

'I'm glad I had you with me today,' he said. 'It

made all the difference. But I'm sorry you were in the crash. I don't like that one bit.'

'We had no choice over what happened and who we were with. But having you by my side made it easier to cope. You took everything so calmly.'

'Much like you.' She'd have been tough no matter who'd been with her, but he'd take her words to heart and enjoy them. Because he believed her. He believed *in* her. She wasn't lying, or trying to earn points to cash in on something he could provide her with later.

Remorse struck. His old cautions were still in place and, unless he let them go, there wasn't going to be a later. He might have to be careful going ahead if he was to avoid more heartbreak, but he had to learn to trust. It wasn't fair on Leesa, or anyone, if he didn't. That was like expecting her to turn out to be another Ellie.

Yeah, he sighed. He was falling for this amazing woman. Falling harder than the chopper hitting the ground earlier. Hopefully Leesa didn't break anything inside him. Or he didn't do the same to her.

Bright lights shone through the carnage from the hovering chopper. The noise was deafening. Handy since he'd run out of things to say without putting his foot in it and telling Leesa the thoughts tripping through his mind. He wasn't ready to divulge where his feelings were at. Not yet. Slowly was the only way to go. If at all.

So, he went with practical, carefully leaning close to shout, 'We need to start moving out of this wreckage.'

Leesa was getting up on her knees when Kevin appeared, holding out his hands to pull her through the narrow space.

Then she was gone and it was his turn. Holding his breath, in an effort to keep the pain under some form of control, he shuffled through to where Kevin reached out for him.

He shook his head. 'No.' Being hauled upright would be agony. It wasn't so great doing it all by himself either. What he hadn't mentioned to Leesa was his ankle was in a bad way too. Hopefully only sprained and not fractured. Whichever, walking wasn't going to be fun.

Kevin led them through the scrub and up to where their rescue helicopter had landed, helping Leesa through the rough terrain, turning back regularly to make sure Nick was with them.

Nick hobbled along, biting his tongue to keep the groans to himself. When Kevin reached to help him into the chopper he didn't refuse. He knew when he was being stubborn for the sake of it. Within minutes Kevin had settled him in a seat and buckled him in, then the chopper was lifting off the ground.

'How're you doing?' Leesa asked.

Nick opened his eyes and stared straight into hers. 'Glad we're out of there.'

'What's wrong with your left foot?'

'Think I've sprained the ankle.'

'Not likely considering you were sitting down when we hit the ground. Most likely a fracture.' She was unclipping her seatbelt, in paramedic mode.

'Leave it, Leesa,' he snapped. 'I'm fine sitting here. The doctors will sort it out when we get to hospital.'

Her head shot up. 'I'm only trying to help,' she snapped back.

'I know. I don't like the situation, that's all.'

'What situation? I thought we were getting along fine.'

Too well, if the thumping in his chest was an indicator. 'We are. But it has been a bit of a wake-up call.'

As she kept staring at him, her face filled with worry. But finally, she said, 'That's understandable. We've had one hell of a shock. It's all catching up with us now we're on our way to hospital.'

He suddenly felt exhausted. 'Certainly is.'

'Yep.' Her smile was tentative.

He took her hand in his. It was becoming his go-to move when he wanted to be close to Leesa. Which it shouldn't if he was serious about backing off. Dropping her hand, he leaned his head back against the seat and closed his eyes to wait out the time till they landed.

'Wake up.' Leesa was shaking him gently.

He jerked upright, groaning as pain slammed under his ribs. 'Have we landed?' The door was opening and bright lights filled the cabin. Guess that was a yes.

Kevin appeared from forward. 'We have. Let's get you two inside to ED. Ma and Pa are in the waiting room. Pacing the floor to oblivion, I imagine.'

'Did anyone pick up Baxter?' Leesa asked. 'I didn't think to ask you to tell Mum. What sort of doggy mum does that make me?'

'One who had a lot else going on in her head,' Kevin told her. 'Your boy's fine. He's in Dad's truck, chewing on a bone, I'm told.'

'That's good. He's used to me being late, but not to turn up at all will have freaked him out.'

'Hate to tell you this, but Dad says he's fine. Karin was about to take him home with her as she figured you were on a callout. Come on, let's get this over and done with.' Kevin helped Leesa out, then turned to give Nick a hand.

'There's a wheelchair coming for you,' Kevin told him.

'How...' Oh, Leesa. Of course she'd have got Kevin to call ahead. 'Thanks.'

Looking into those beautiful but tired eyes, his head and heart were all over the place. He did want more with her. That much he was not going to deny any longer. What was the point? He knew he was done for. But that didn't mean he was ready to rush in. After what had happened, the caution had grown even bigger and he wasn't totally sure why. So forget backing off, and try going slowly.

'I'm discharging you,' the ED doctor told Leesa. 'You were quite right. Lots of bruising that you'll know about for days to come, but nothing more serious.'

'Thanks, Laurie.' She wasn't going anywhere until she knew if Nick would be kept in overnight. She swung her legs off the bed and gasped when her thighs protested. 'Painful bruises.'

'The result of severe impact,' Laurie nodded. 'Take it easy for the next couple of days. Stay away from work.'

'I'll see that she does,' Joy answered before Leesa could argue. 'The same goes for you, Nick.'

Joy had turned up within minutes of the chopper delivering them to the hospital. She hadn't been allowed to see Mark, who had had a brain bleed and was now in ICU.

'I'm not arguing,' Nick growled as he lay

sprawled on the bed in the next cubicle, looking shattered.

'Is Nick staying overnight?' she asked Laurie.

'I see no reason for that once we've finished with him,' the doctor grinned.

'Just as well or we'd have argued,' Nick told Laurie.

His X-rays had shown four broken ribs and a fracture in his wrist, none in his swollen ankle. He'd been right on that score. Thankfully, as they'd thought, his lung hadn't been punctured. That was the best result. It would've been horrifying if that had happened. There was nothing she'd have been able to do to help him other than keep him on oxygen, and with a hole in his lung that'd have been an exercise in futility.

Her chest tightened. She could've lost Nick. And she wasn't thinking of a work colleague. No, this was the man who had ignored her boundaries and walked right on into her head and heart. Throw in his injuries and she was going to insist he come back to her place.

'Nick, a nurse is going to put your wrist in a soft cast. You'll have it on for a week then, when the swelling's gone down, it will be replaced with a plaster version,' Laurie told him.

He was looking at Laurie as if it was hard to understand what she was saying. 'Then I'm free to go, too?'

'Yes. Nothing we can do about your ribs except prescribe strong analgesics, along with antibiotics for that cut on your chin I stitched. *And*—' she emphasised the word '—I insist you don't get too physical. For the sake of your ribs and that ankle.'

'The pain will keep me in line.'

Leesa blinked. He was admitting that? Showed how everything had got to him, because normally he was averse to revealing his feelings.

A nurse slipped into the cubicle. 'Nick? I'm Enid and I'm here to sort out your left wrist.'

Then Kevin strode into her cubicle. It was getting like a circus in here, but rescue staff were given more leeway than general patients because of what they did for people.

'Hey, sis, how're you doing?'

'All good. I can go home any time I like.'

'That's what I was hoping. I'll take you home when you're ready. What about you, Nick?'

'I'll be on my way as soon as this cast's on.'

Leesa said, 'Come back to my place, Nick. You don't want to be on your own tonight.' She didn't want to be alone. The crash had been horrendous, and now that they were safe and sorted, she was beginning to feel more shaken than when they'd first hit the ground. Her parents would be happy for her to go to their house, but she wanted her own place with her own things around her. And

Nick with her too, because he'd understand how she felt. He'd been through it too.

'Nick?'

He was looking at her as though he wasn't sure what to do. Finally, he nodded. 'Okay. Thank you.'

She couldn't decide if he was happy going home with her or merely agreeing because being on his own wasn't a good option at the moment, but now wasn't the time to delve deeper. They were beyond making sense after all that had happened.

'Good idea, Leesa,' said Kevin. 'What about some clean clothes, Nick? You look like something the butcher chopped up.'

'Tactful. Could we swing by my apartment?' Nick asked.

'Only if I go in and get what you want. I don't think it's a good idea for you to move around any more than necessary,' Kevin told him.

Nick looked from him to her, and Leesa laughed. 'Don't even think about arguing.' She sensed he was on the verge of doing exactly that and it bugged her, though she didn't know why.

'With a Bennett? Not likely.' Then he turned serious. 'Thanks, but—'

She cut him off. 'But nothing. It makes sense for you to be with someone tonight.' Her heart dipped. Was something wrong? She'd have to wait to find out. She was shattered and could barely string a sentence together.

'I don't want to be a nuisance when you're a train wreck too, but you're right, Leesa. I'd feel more comfortable knowing you're there.'

That wasn't so hard, was it? 'Good. Let's get out of here.'

CHAPTER EIGHT

NICK LOOKED AROUND HIM. He'd thought as it was Leesa's grandmother's house it would be small, but it was huge. The lounge he sat in was the size of a football field. Okay, a small one toddlers played on, but it was still large. Light and airy with big bay windows that looked out over what appeared to be an expansive lawn and flower gardens. Someone had forgotten to turn the outside lights off.

'Who does the gardens?' he asked Leesa. 'They're stunning.'

'I do. Gran set them up over many years, and when I moved in I couldn't let them go to ruin.'

'You like gardening?' Of course she did. It was pretty darned obvious. 'You must if you keep them in such good order.' So this was one of her interests outside of work. Probably the most dominant one, given the size of the plots.

'I get a thrill out of planting a shrub or bulb and seeing the result when it blooms.' She was sitting on a leather rocker with her legs stretched out on the foot rest, a plate of the fried chicken and salad her mother had prepared for them on her knees.

'I wouldn't know a bulb from a shrub,' he muttered. Gardens came with homes.

'There's always time to learn.'

'You know what? You're right.' He was thinking about having a garden? Where? If he got a dog, he'd said he'd move, so how about a place with a lawn *and* a garden? 'I might give it a go sometime.'

'Sometime?'

'Okay, if I move from the apartment, I could be tempted to look into buying a house with a small yard.'

'If?'

'Will you stop questioning everything I say?' He'd just told her what he was thinking of doing and she kept at him, wanting to know more. Frustrating to say the least, because he was so unsure of his next step, of how to follow through on the love he held for her.

He snapped. 'It's new for me to be talking about this. I need to get my head around it.' It was huge to even be thinking about stopping his nomadic life to settle in one place, even more so to tell Leesa what he thought. Although he couldn't guarantee how long for. He had a feeling that if he started on this change of lifestyle he might adhere to it—because he might've found what he'd spent most of his life looking for. The only thing wrong there was he was worried about hurting Leesa if he failed. He needed to toughen up and make some decisions, not drag it out because his heart was involved.

'I'm trying to support you in a backward kind of way.' Leesa bit into a drumstick and chewed thoughtfully. 'I can't imagine what it's been like not to have a house to call home, where gardens, decorating, renovations are all part of everyday things to attend to. You've missed out on a hell of a lot.'

She never minced her words.

He should be thankful, but sometimes they came too close to be easily accepted. Tonight, he'd try. He and Leesa had been through a traumatic experience together and needed to put it behind them without arguing. Now he thought about it, his reaction to her questions might be because he'd felt so out of sorts since the crash.

No, there was more to it than that. He was out of sorts because he'd woken up to the fact that he loved Leesa. Which was downright scary. There was a lot at stake.

'You're right, I have, but I do not want you feeling sorry for me.'

'I don't. I admire how you've got on with your life, and seem to be starting to look for what it is you really want.'

She read him well. Too well, if he was honest. No one had ever done that like she did. Except Patrick, and that had turned out good for him. Did that mean Leesa could be good for him if he stayed around? Frightening. It could mean everything, or it could turn to dust because he wasn't sure he understood how to make it work well.

'It's taken years but you're right, I have started thinking of my future and not my past.' If that wasn't huge then what was? Falling in love most definitely was. As would giving his heart freely. Those would be the final winners. And the largest hurdles. He'd nearly lost her today, and that scared the pants off him. Others had left him in the past. For that to happen again—well, he had no idea how he'd get through that. Yet he wanted so much to try to make it work with Leesa.

'I'm pleased for you, Nick. Everyone deserves happiness.'

Says she who'd struggled to put her past behind her. They really were two peas in the proverbial pod. 'Including you.'

'What's more, we shouldn't sit around waiting for happiness to arrive. We should get on and make it happen.' Leesa was watching him closely, no doubt looking for a reaction to that statement.

And he had one he'd love to share. She was his dream woman. He was making inroads into getting on with living life to the full. He opened his mouth to speak, closed it again. One thing to think how he felt, quite another to tell Leesa.

What if he'd misunderstood her and she didn't want anything more than a friendship with him? What if, when she said everyone was entitled to be happy, she only meant he was too, and wasn't saying it would be with her? The mistakes he'd made in the past reared their ugly heads and shut him down.

'I see.' She stood up slowly, wincing with pain all the way.

He got to his feet even more slowly, the throbbing in his ribs diabolical. But the pounding in his heart was more painful. He had to keep Leesa onside, and the only way to go was by being open with her as much as he dared, so they could at least talk more.

'No, Leesa, you don't. I haven't explained myself. I know that. It doesn't come easily for me, but that's not a good excuse. Spending time with you is a priority. I always feel the best I have in a long time, if not for ever, when I'm with you.'

'I can live with that for now.' Her crooked smile showed how exhausted she was. Holding out her hand to him, she added, 'Let's go to bed. I'm shattered, and you look no better.'

'Your mother made up a spare bed for me.'

Leesa blinked. 'You're serious? There's a surprise. I'd have thought she'd have locked the doors to the spare bedrooms so you had to join me.'

So Jodi liked him being with her daughter. His heart swelled. Another good thing to happen. Except if he let Leesa down, in any way, he'd be letting down her family as well. 'Could she be thinking I need to be very careful in bed right now?'

'Definitely.' Taking his hand, she tugged him gently. 'We can share a bed without getting active.' Another blink. 'I'd say that'll be difficult, but right now all I want is to be stretched out and comfortable so I can sleep. Not very sexy, I know.' She shrugged.

He laughed lightly, aware of not moving his chest too much. 'It's about all I'll be able to manage.' As he followed Leesa through the house, he noted three spare bedrooms with perfectly arranged furniture. 'Which bedroom would Jodi have chosen for me?'

'The one on your right. It's the second largest and the one I use for visitors if I have any.'

'Not many then?' He'd have thought with her caring, friendly manner she'd always have someone dropping by for a night or two.

'Most of my friends live around here.' She didn't sound sad.

'Where does Baxter usually sleep?'

'Where do you think?'

'Your bedroom.' Where else would she have him? This was Leesa, the soft-hearted dog mum. Baxter was with Leesa's parents, as everyone thought it would give Leesa a chance to sleep and not be nudged in those painful places.

'I'm going to have a shower. If you want one, there's a bathroom further along the hall. Towels are in the drawer beneath the basin.'

'Sounds idyllic. Hot water to soak away the grime and loosen my muscles.'

Leesa spun around to face him and gritted her teeth. 'Ow.' Her chest rose as she drew in a deep breath. 'Silly girl. Do you want a hand getting your shirt off? I can't imagine it'll be a picnic.'

'Yes, please.' It'd be the first time she'd removed his clothes without him getting hard.

Her grin told him she'd read his mind. 'Who'd have thought?'

'Not me.'

'Now that you're in my room you can use the ensuite. You can fall out of the shower and into bed with only a few steps. I'll use the main bathroom.' She was already turning the sheets back.

He hated that she was taking so much care of him, but right now he didn't have the energy to argue. After being settled in that comfortable chair in the lounge, walking down the hallway had taken a lot of effort, with pain ricocheting around his body in all directions. 'You're a gem.'

'And you hate being in this situation. I get that.' Heading into the ensuite, she took a towel off a shelf and laid it on the counter. 'There you go. See you in bed shortly.'

Still no reaction from his body. He really was a mess. Hopefully he'd be able to cuddle into her long, warm frame and fall asleep holding her with the arm on his good side.

Leesa stood under the hot water and let the heat soak into her bruised and battered body. It was wonderful. Never mind she'd be too hot and probably sweat some when she got out. Right now, she needed this to relax her muscles, which were tight and damned sore. That crash landing had been horrific, jarring every part of her body. But she was grateful that's all she'd suffered.

Nick hadn't been so lucky.

As for Mark, he was gravely ill and would be for a while to come, by the sound of it. Brain bleeds were no picnic.

It all went to show you didn't have a clue what a day would bring when you got up in the morning.

She shampooed and conditioned her hair, then realised she'd have to waste time drying it before she could crawl in beside Nick. But she couldn't have left it as it was when she felt dirty from top to toe. Now she was deliciously clean. Finally flicking the water off, she grabbed her towel and dried off, feeling so much better.

She was spending the night in *her* bed with Nick. It was the first time he'd come to the house, and it was another step forward in their relationship. He'd seemed concerned he'd given too much away earlier, but for her it was progress. It meant he trusted her, and she felt special that he had talked about how he was changing, because she wasn't holding back any longer.

Nick was lying on his back when she returned to her room. 'How's that working?' she asked.

'Not bad.' There was a familiar twinkle in his eyes.

'Oh, no. We are behaving tonight.' No way would she have Nick in pain from anything they got up to.

'Hate to say it but you're right. I can lie on my right side though. You can back in so we can cuddle.'

'Sounds perfect. I think I'll be asleep in thirty seconds flat.' Which meant missing out on feeling his arm around her. 'I'll do my best to stay awake for a while.'

'Don't even try. We both need sleep more than anything.' He rolled carefully onto his good side.

Leesa slipped under the sheet and leaned over to kiss him. 'What a day. Good night.' Moving carefully, she turned onto her side, back towards him and smiled as their bodies came together. His skin was warm and his breath tickled the back of her neck. Sheer bliss.

'Leesa. Wake up.' A hand was shaking her. 'Wake up, Leesa.' It was Nick's voice.

Dragging her eyes open, she stared around the dark room, feeling cold and shaky. 'Where am I?'

'In your bed. I think you were having a nightmare.'

It came rushing back. 'The chopper crashing. The trees hitting us. You unable to move. Me hurting.' She gulped air. 'It was awful.'

Nick wound an arm around her, beneath her breasts, tucking her close. 'Going through it once was bad enough.'

'That's put me off wanting to sleep.' She couldn't keep reliving the nightmare. It was awful. 'At least we're no worse off than we were the first time.' Her mouth tasted of bile. 'Have you slept?'

'A little. I wake every time I move.'

'Time for some more analgesics.' Except she didn't want to leave the safety of Nick's arms. Shaking her head, she admonished herself. Not safety, comfort. She *was* safe. It was her head causing problems now. 'I'll get them in a moment.'

'I can get them.'

She sat up immediately. 'No, Nick. That'd

mean more pain for you. I'll get some for myself too.' They'd ease the aches and might drag her under to sleep, even if she fought it.

After they'd taken the tablets, Nick lay on his back and Leesa stretched out beside him, holding his hand. She felt her heart melting for Nick. He'd opened up some more during their wait in the chopper. Could the crash have been something good in disguise?

Staring upward, the tension that started from the moment Mark shouted they were in trouble slipped away at last, leaving her languid and comfortable. Nick was her dream man. She trusted him completely. He'd never deliberately hurt her. Was he falling for her? More than anything she hoped so. For now, she'd go with the flow. She was too tired for anything else.

It had been the strangest day of her life, yet she was happy. Yes, happy to have found this man. All she had to do now was make him understand they could have a future together. But not tonight. Tonight was for unwinding and being comfortable together without firing up the lust and getting hot. They needed to be able to share time that didn't involve sex, only love. And if Nick wasn't into loving her then she'd deal with that another day. Right now, she was happy to roll with her own feelings.

Shuffling closer to him, she laid a hand on his

chest and closed her eyes. This was near perfect. If she didn't move too much and set off the aches.

'Time I got back to work,' Joy said as she stood up the next day after dropping by to see how they were doing. 'Glad you're both feeling a bit better.'

'I'll be back on the job tomorrow,' Leesa told her. 'Thanks for the filled bread rolls. They were delicious.'

'You're welcome.' Joy paused, looked from her to Nick. 'Does the accident change either of your minds re my job? Last week's interviews went well I hear.'

'The job's the last thing on my mind at the moment,' Leesa told her.

'I'm in,' Nick told Joy.

'If one of you gets the job is the other going to throw their toys out of the cot?' Joy asked.

'Not at all.'

'No way.' Leesa glanced at Nick, then back to Joy. 'My concern is how the rest of the staff will see it. They might read too much into situations where say I give Nick a job to do that someone else wanted, and vice versa.'

Nick was watching her closely. Looking for what? She was only putting the truth out there.

'We're a small crew compared to ambulance stations you've worked in previously, Leesa. We're close. I've never had any problem with any member thinking they should've been given a job over someone else. I can't see it happening if either of you take my place.' Joy was focused completely on her. 'I know you well, and I can't see you giving Nick, or anyone else, more than their fair share of the good jobs. It's not like you.'

Her heart softened at the compliment. 'Thank you. I should've talked to you sooner, then I could've stopped worrying.'

'So your application remains in place?'

'Yes. I don't know if I'll be comfortable flying in choppers any more. Spending time in the office seems far safer.'

Nick watched Leesa as she made a plunger of coffee. She looked thoughtful, as though he'd done something wrong applying for Joy's position. 'You still okay with us competing for the same job? First time we've come up against each other.'

'Interesting area to be doing so.' Her finger was scratching at the hem of her shorts, where a huge bruise covered most of her thigh. It had to be painful but she never mentioned it, or any of the others he'd noticed during the night.

'Look, Leesa, if you're really worried about being my boss—' he paused and gave her a smile '—I promise to behave.'

His smile hadn't worked. She looked unsettled. 'I am nervous about flying now.'

He tried another smile. 'That's natural but you'll get over it.'

'You don't know that.'

'I know you. You're tough.'

'Is this you trying to talk me out of trying for the job?' The spoon she'd been holding slammed onto the bench.

Nick came straight back. 'Not at all. I don't need you to do that to make me feel more optimistic.' Why were they even talking about this? It hadn't been an issue before, as far as he knew.

Her head shot up. 'I know that. You'd be brilliant as chief of operations.'

Knock him down. Now he was confused. 'Thank you, but so would you.'

Her mouth twitched. 'We're doing well so far. Everything feels like a big deal at the moment, probably as a result of what happened yesterday.'

Just like that the angst left him. 'Good idea. Who gets the job's not up to us anyway.'

'We won't be the only applicants.'

'True.' If he got the position it would be a step forward in changing his life. He'd be stopping in one place. The place where Leesa lived. Could he do it?

'What are you thinking now?' she asked. 'I can't read you.'

Leesa never let him away with a thing. 'I'm wondering what it would be like to live in one place for more than a year or two. To settle down permanently.' If yesterday had taught him anything it was that he loved Leesa to bits. The ramifications were huge after he'd lost others he'd loved. What if he lost Leesa? He'd lost too many people who were important to him already.

'Nick, before you go any further, hear me out.'

His chest was tightening. What was coming next? He should leave before his heart was shattered. Or before she showed how much she expected of him. But it wasn't that easy. He cared too much. He wanted to believe they could make this happen, he just didn't trust life to give him a chance.

'Meeting you has been the best thing to happen to me in a long time.' Her gaze was steady.

His heart wrenched at her words. But there was something in her voice that said there was more to come. 'Carry on.'

'Like you, I have problems from my past.'

He gasped. 'You think I'd bully you? No damned way. How can you even begin to think that?'

'The same way you feel about settling down and trying to make a life for yourself. I want to follow my instincts but they've got me into trouble before.'

The anger disappeared. 'I get that. Believe me,

I would never pressure you to do something for me that you didn't want to.'

'I know that. Truly. It's just that—' She stopped, hauled in a huge breath. 'I'm scared. I've fallen for you, Nick.'

This time it felt as though his heart had stopped. 'Leesa—'

Her hand went up in a stop sign. 'Wait. I've spent years not believing I could find a man who'd treat me well and accept me for who I am. A man to love for ever and have children with, to establish a loving environment for a family. I have finally found him—you. Despite what I've just said it is you.' Her breasts rose on a deep breath. There was more to come.

He waited, heart in his throat.

'I know you still struggle with trust, or admitting you might be there now. I'm taking a huge leap here, but this is my heart speaking, so if you're not interested then please tell me.'

His mouth dried. His head spun with what she'd told him. She loved him. He loved her, but how to tell her when he couldn't put the past completely behind him? Ellie had said she loved him and look what she'd done.

Leesa's not Ellie.

She'd never play around behind his back. She'd tell him outright if she'd stopped loving him. He'd had a lifetime of learning not to trust people, which led to him not trusting himself, hence wanting to step back from Leesa before he hurt her. 'I don't know what to say.'

After the crash he'd thought he could walk away to save them both from more hurt. Now it seemed he was wrong. He couldn't turn his back on her for any reason.

So talk to her—speak from your heart.

Therein lay the problem. He didn't know how to. The last time he'd done that it had come back to wreck his heart.

Silence fell between them.

Finally Leesa stood up and crossed to look out the window at the garden beyond. After a few minutes she turned, and the sadness in her face shocked him. 'You don't believe you're ready. I get that. If I'm putting pressure on you, it's because I think you are ready to make the changes you've been looking for.'

She paused, fidgeting with her hair. 'It's obvious you need some space, and I'm pushing you. I've told you my feelings. I don't want to hear anything you don't one hundred per cent believe.' She shoved a hand through her hair and sighed. 'Or I've just made a complete fool of myself.'

'Leesa, it's not that.' Her family had stood by him last night, and brought home the fact that if he was involved with Leesa he was also involved with them. They'd share their lives with him. They'd also have him for dog tucker if he hurt her. And he couldn't trust himself not to. He had no experience of true loving family. Messing up would not be hard.

She waited, her foot tapping the cork tiles.

What to say? What to say?

Finally Leesa shook her head at him and said, 'Go away, Nick, and think long and hard about what you're really looking for. You can't go to work at the moment, so use the time to sort yourself out. If I'm not going to be in the picture then let me know sooner rather than later.'

His heart was breaking as he watched her walk out of the room, her head high and back ramrod straight. His heart tightened for this amazing woman, who he was already hurting. She was strong, and not afraid to show him.

'Goodbye, Leesa.'

For now. She was right about one thing. He had to sort himself out, starting now. When he did tell her he loved her there couldn't be any hesitation. No looking back. It would be an all or nothing decision. He wanted all.

He pulled his phone from his pocket to call a taxi. Leesa was right about one thing—he had decisions to make, and the sooner the better for both of them.

She'd told him she loved him. Hope was flapping around inside his chest like a stranded fish.

He'd followed her here on a whim, which he hadn't been able to admit to himself until recently. They'd happily reconnected and had been getting along well. Now he had to find the courage to follow his heart.

The taxi pulled up and he got in, taking a long look at Leesa's home with him.

CHAPTER NINE

'WELCOME BACK, LEESA,' Jess said and got up from the table to give her a careful hug. 'Love the colours on your face.'

'I'm going to scare my patients, for sure.' Leesa filled a mug from the coffee plunger. Everyone was here, as if they'd been waiting for her.

'How are you feeling?' Darren asked. 'Apart from sore all over.'

Heartbroken. I haven't heard from Nick for nearly two days.

'Wary of helicopters, but otherwise ready to get back in the seat.' Planes seemed a whole lot safer at the moment.

'Here's the thing,' Darren said. 'The helicopter didn't fail. Mark did, and I'm not being nasty about that. The poor blighter had a serious medical issue.'

'He did an amazing job getting us so close to the ground before he lost consciousness. That's what Nick and I think happened anyway. We owe him, for sure. But I still think I might find my first ride in a chopper a little scary.'

'I don't doubt that for a moment,' Darren agreed.

'How's Nick doing?' Jess asked. 'Joy says he's not coming back to work for ten days or so. Lifting trolleys or boards with patients on will be a no-no for quite a while.'

Ten days? Her heart sank. That was longer than Laurie had said was necessary. So he wasn't in a rush to see her and become a part of her life. He could've done other less physical jobs. 'Broken ribs are nasty by all accounts.'

'They hurt like hell with every little move you make,' one of the paramedics said. 'Speaking from experience after a particularly rough rugby game years back.'

'He could do the paperwork and let Joy have some air time,' Darren noted, unaware he was on the same track as Leesa.

'Hey, good to see you.' Joy walked in carrying a plate with a large chocolate cake. 'Here's to you, Leesa, and having you back on board.'

She stared at Joy. 'A cake? Chocolate too.' She wiped a hand over her eyes. 'You're spoiling me.'

Placing the plate on the table, Joy gave her a gentle hug. 'You gave us a huge fright, you three.'

Leesa swallowed down the lump in her throat. She hadn't given much thought to how everyone else would've felt when they heard the chopper had gone down. Just knew they'd have been in a hurry to help them. 'Thanks, guys.' She reached for a tissue and blew her nose. So unlike her to get emotional in front of people. 'We'd better put some aside for Nick and Mark.'

Joy handed her a knife and some plates. 'Nope. They get their own cakes when they return.'

Nick might miss out altogether, she thought as she cut into the layered cake, if he chose to move on yet again. He had said goodbye to her, not see you at work. Should she call him and ask how he was doing?

No. She'd said she'd give him space and she had to stick to that. The last thing she needed to do was upset him all over again. But she missed him more than she could believe. Every minute of the day and night. Listening out for him, looking for his ute in the driveway, holding the pillow he'd used, burying her face into it and breathing in his scent. Pure male with a hint of spice. The best smell in the universe. Her universe anyway.

'Here, get your teeth into this.' Joy had taken over cutting slices of cake and plating up. 'When we've finished here, I'd like a moment of your time, unless a call out comes in.'

Her stomach sank. Time to face reality. 'No problem.' *Liar.*

The cake sat heavily in her stomach when she went into Joy's office. Had Joy heard from Nick? Had he handed in his notice and was in the throes of leaving town?

'Wipe that grim expression off your face, Leesa. I'm not here to make things difficult for you.' Joy took a seat opposite her. 'I want to re-iterate that I believe you and Nick can work together if one of you has my role.'

If Nick comes back to me. Or comes back at all.

'You haven't heard from him?'

'Only to say he wanted a few more days off than originally agreed on when we discussed his injuries.' Joy was watching her closely. 'Is there something more to this?'

'Not really. Nick has some sorting out to do.' She'd spent a lot of time since he'd gone considering her future with or without him in it, and had realised changing roles at work wasn't what would make her happy. Even if Nick didn't want to be a part of her life, she now knew she wanted to make more of her life outside work. Clenching her hands in her lap, she returned Joy's steady gaze. 'I'm withdrawing my application as of now.'

'Can I ask why?'

'I've been too focused on work and it's time I had some other interests. Apart from Gran's gardens,' she added with a small smile.

'What if I told you the board members are going to offer you the job?'

Her eyes widened. 'Seriously?' Pride filled her. She was thrilled, but it didn't change a thing. 'That's amazing, but sorry, I won't be changing my mind again.' She wasn't tempted at all. 'Sorry to muck you all around.'

'You haven't. We've a firm second contender.' Joy stood up. Conversation over. 'But I admit I'd have loved seeing you in my role. You'd have been great at it. Maybe at a later date.'

Somehow, she doubted that. Her pride grew though. It was good to hear she was appreciated. 'I'd better get to work. And Joy, thanks for being so patient.'

Walking out to the plane she couldn't help thinking about what lay ahead. The fact was she didn't have a clue, and for once that didn't worry her. Except when it came to Nick, and that was out of her hands. He'd come back to her or he wouldn't. It was beyond hard waiting to find out, and for every hour she did her heart cracked open a little wider. It was going to be decimating if he didn't, but better now than further on. Damn it, it was already bad enough that she struggled with getting on with all her jobs.

But she would. She was strong. She'd made a decision to show Nick her love for him. If it backfired, she could still feel relieved she'd done all she could.

But was it enough? That was the burning question.

Nick's finger hovered over the 'pay now' icon. The air ticket to Adelaide was a mere tap away.

Did he really need to visit Patrick and talk about his feelings for Leesa, to explain why he was in such a quandary? He already knew what the judge would say. *'Get on with following your dream and stop wasting your life.'* Patrick wouldn't come up with any new answers to the questions filling his head.

Leaning back in his chair, Nick looked around the apartment and sighed. The same old same old. No different to every apartment he'd lived in over the years since graduating. The views altered, as did the room sizes, wall colours, floor levels. In other words, unexciting, uninteresting. A place to sleep at the end of a shift, no more, no less. He was over it, and ready to move somewhere permanent. In Cairns. With Leesa. She meant everything to him.

'See, I don't need to talk to Patrick. I know what to do.'

There would be no avoiding the truth any longer.

He was ready to settle down and try to make a go of having a home life. A full life, not one focused entirely on being a doctor.

There. The truth. And he wanted to do it all with Leesa. He wanted to love her freely, with no fear of letting her down or hurting her. He understood life didn't run that smoothly all the time though. People had to take chances. Including him.

His phone played the tune to the dance he and Leesa had got up close and personal to in Brisbane. The caller ID was unknown.

'Hello?'

'Nick, mate, it's Kevin. How're you doing?'

Why was Leesa's brother calling him? 'I'm good.'

'Those ribs still giving you grief?'

'Unfortunately, yes. What've you been up to?' What was this about? Who gave Kevin his number? Leesa? He doubted it. She'd been adamant about no contact until he'd made up his mind about their future. She wouldn't involve her brother in this.

'I'm heading out on the boat for a few days to catch a load of prawn tomorrow and thought I'd check in on you before I go. Is there anything I can do for you?'

Knock him down. This wasn't a seek and tell call. Kevin was being as decent as the rest of his family. Not really surprising. 'No, all good here. But thanks for the offer. We should catch up for a beer when you get back.' See? Small steps.

'There's a plan. Once those ribs are up to scratch I'm taking you out on the boat for a couple of days, show you how we catch your favourite food.'

Staying here was sounding better and better. 'I'd enjoy that. How's Leesa doing?' he asked without thought. Because she was constantly on his mind. Because she just never went away.

'You should ask her yourself,' Kevin told him. Then relented. 'She's back at work and seems to be recovering from the battering she took.'

That was a relief. 'I'm glad to hear that.'

'Talk to her, man. She's missing you.'

So Kevin knew they weren't in touch, which probably meant so did Jodi and Brent. 'I have to get a few things in order first. I don't want to hurt her by rushing it.'

'Don't take too long. I'll give you a buzz about that drink when I get back at the beginning of next week. See ya.' The guy was gone.

On the laptop the 'pay now' icon had disappeared, replaced with 'time's up'.

Time's up. How appropriate. The decision was made. He was staying. He loved Leesa beyond measure. It was what he was going to do about it that needed fixing. And he knew the answer to that too.

For the first time since the crash a cold beer beckoned. Getting a bottle from the fridge he headed out onto his balcony. He leaned on the balustrade and stared out at central Cairns and the airport beyond. His new home town. The feeling of achievement over reaching his decision filled him with contentment.

Kevin calling to see how he was doing made him feel good. Like he belonged somehow. And while that had worried him, now he grabbed it, accepted it. All because of one amazing woman he'd sat down beside at a party in Brisbane over a year ago, he'd found what he'd wanted for so long. Leesa and love, things he could not walk away from. Ever.

Kevin had raised the subject of Leesa. It sounded as though he knew more than he was letting on. He couldn't imagine Leesa talking about him to the family, but then they knew her well and would have figured out something was up.

The dance tune rang again. He never got this many calls.

This time it was Joy. 'What's up, boss?'

'You have a new job. Congratulations.'

His heart stopped. Did he want this? 'What about Leesa?'

'She pulled out.'

'When?' *Why?*

'Yesterday. I'll leave it to Leesa to explain why.'

Had he said 'why' out loud? She'd better not have done it for his sake. He didn't want that and it would make him very uncomfortable.

'I'm—' What was he? Only a couple of days ago he was going to retract his application. But now that he had made up his mind to stay in Cairns, climbing the career ladder was a start to settling in and making that life with Leesa he so desperately wanted. 'Do you want me to come in and go through everything?'

'You're on sick leave. We'll talk when you're back on duty. And Nick?'

'Yes?'

'I won't tell the rest of the crew until you've had a couple of days to think about it.'

Joy got that he had concerns. But he didn't. He was ready. 'I don't need to think about it, but I'd appreciate you keeping quiet for now. I'd like to talk to Leesa first.'

'Fair enough.'

'Thanks again. Have you got someone covering for me?'

'We're managing. Everyone's pulling their weight and making sure Leesa doesn't overdo it. She might say she's fine, but she struggles with lifting bags, let alone patients.'

Of course Leesa would be downplaying her pain. There was no arguing with her—ever. 'Right, I'll see you on Monday. I don't need those extra days I asked for any more.' He didn't need Patrick to tell him what he already knew.

After finishing the call he stared at the laptop as ideas of what to do next bounced into his mind. He got another beer and sat down to study the real estate options for the area.

Rural or beach? Definitely not in the city. That wouldn't suit Leesa, nor him, now he was coming to understand how much he wanted this. As different to boring apartments as possible for starters. Space for Baxter and the dog he intended getting.

He was getting ahead of himself. Leesa liked living in her grandmother's house and might not want to shift. Only one way to find out, and in the meantime he'd do all he could to get this happening. She'd said she had fallen for him. He could not let her down—ever. He trusted her with his heart. He really did. So he was going to do everything imaginable to make her happy. And more.

There was a buzz in his veins. This was the most exciting thing he'd ever done. He was finally coming home.

Leesa dragged herself through the front door, glad to be home and that the week was over. First stop—the fridge, and a glass of pinot blanc to unwind. The days at work since the accident had been tiring and her heart hadn't been in it.

It had been tied up with Nick, as she wondered if he was still in town or if he'd already packed his bags, headed away to the next city on his radar.

Baxter raced through the house, headed for the kitchen and his food bowl.

Okay, the wine came second to dog roll and biscuits. 'Give me a minute, boy.'

Wag, wag. His tail swished back and forth on the floor.

Her heart expanded at the sight of his face full of hope and love. Dogs were so easy to please. She adored him.

The door chime sounded.

Baxter was off in a blur, tail still wagging, no hackles up.

Who would be calling in now? Not any of her family. They walked in like it was home to them, which in a way it was.

'Hey, boy, how are you?'

Her heart leapt. Nick. Baxter had known. Was this good or bad?

'Leesa? Are you there?'

'Coming.' Slowly.

Suddenly she was afraid. She'd been kidding herself if she thought she'd cope with Nick saying he wanted nothing more to do with her. Her skin tightened and bumps lifted on her arms. Rubbing them hard she made her way back to the door. And Nick.

'Hey, Leesa.' Nick stood tall and confident, a bunch of tulips in his hand. Not a clue to what he was going to tell her. The flowers could be a closing gift. His confidence might be because he'd made some decisions he was happy with that didn't include her. 'I've missed you.' His eyes were full of love, or so she wanted to believe.

Her heart was pounding like a drummer, like it knew that was love streaming her way. Locking her eyes with Nick's, she whispered. 'I've missed you too.'

He didn't move. 'Leesa, I love you with all my heart.' His voice was firm. But his hand shook as he held out the tulips. 'For you, my darling.'

Nick loved her? Nick loved her. Yes. As she took them, she said, 'My favourite blooms.' Had he known that?

'Jodi told me.'

'You've been talking to Mum?' That had to be good, didn't it? As were the flowers. She couldn't quite take in everything, was still waiting for a catch. 'Come in.' Nick was right behind her as she headed to the kitchen. 'I'm about to pour a wine. Want one?'

'I'd love one. But first there is something else I want to tell you.'

Her heart slowed. Damn it. She was done with guessing. 'What?'

'I'm not moving away. I'm going to be a permanent fixture in Cairns, or around the area anyway. And I want to share that with you.'

'You're staying?' She had to check.

'Yes, I am. I meant it, Leesa. I love you.'

'Oh, wow.'

The tulips got a little crushed in the ensuing hug and kiss.

'Easy,' Nick gasped.

Hell. His ribs. Placing her palm on his cheek, she leaned in to brush a light kiss on his lips. 'I'm sorry. In the heat of the moment, I forgot.'

'So did I.' His laughter sent a thrill of desire pulsing through her.

But they had to restrain themselves. Broken ribs didn't make for active lovemaking. 'Damn.'

'We'll find a way round the problem, I'm sure. But let's start with that wine you mentioned. I built up a thirst coming here, stressing over whether you'd be happy to see me or not.'

'Why wouldn't I? I told you I love you.' Oh, not in quite those words. Placing the flowers on the bench she faced him. 'Nick Springer, I love you with everything I've got. I love you,' she repeated, because she loved saying it.

He reached for her again, held her with a small gap between them and leaned in to kiss her senseless. 'Love you too, Leesa.'

It was Baxter head-knocking her knee that drew her back. 'Okay, boy, I guess you've been patient enough. Nick, you pour the wine while I feed hungry guts here.'

'Sure.' He found the glasses and got the bottle

from the fridge, while watching her feed Baxter then find a vase for the tulips.

'Simply beautiful,' she said as she placed them on the sideboard. 'Let's sit out on the deck.'

'I've been offered Joy's job and I'm taking it,' Nick told her as he sat down beside her on the cane couch. 'I know you withdrew your application.'

'If Mark hadn't been so ill, I'd thank him for the crash and waking me up to a few things.' She sipped the wine and continued. 'I don't want to be in charge of operations. I just want to do an honest day's work helping people and then come home to do other things I enjoy.'

'Like gardening and walking Baxter.'

She nodded. 'And establishing a home that's mine, not keeping Gran's going as hers. She's not coming back here, and I'm ready to be creative with the house and grounds.'

'You want to stay in this house?'

'I haven't got that far with future plans. I was waiting till I heard what you were going to say about us being together.' Loving each other meant living together. It had to or any relationship was off the agenda.

Damn but she loved it when he brushed his lips over her cheek.

'Here's what I've been doing these past few days.' He sat back with a smug look on his face.

'I've been looking at properties for sale north of the city, mostly on the coast and one inland with five acres and the potential to buy the neighbour's.'

'You have?' Her head spun with amazement. 'When you make up your mind you certainly get on with things.'

'About time, don't you think?'

She answered with a kiss. 'So is there a property you prefer above all the others?'

'I'm tossing up between the inland one and a stunning house near Trinity Beach. But I'd like you to see them first. You mightn't like either of them.'

'You're asking for my opinion? Does that mean what I think it does?'

'Of course.' His smile was devastating. 'But here's the big question. Will you go on dates with me? Give us time to get to know each other really well? As in looking forward and seeing what we both want individually and together?'

Her knees weakened as she looked into those beautiful blue eyes. 'Yes, Nick Springer, I will date you. But be warned, I already know what I want and you're a part of it all.'

'Afraid I'll get away?' he grinned before kissing her again.

'Too right,' she managed between kisses. 'Let me warn you, you won't get a chance. I love you too much.'

'Good, because I love you back. And, just so you know, one of the two houses I preferred had five bedrooms, while the other had three.'

'Let's go for five.'

'That means we'll be living by Trinity Beach.'

'Bring it on. Dogs love the seaside.'

Their next kiss sealed the deal.

EPILOGUE

LEESA SPRINGER'S HEART was singing as she gazed into her daughter's eyes. 'You are so beautiful, Courtney.' Tears welled up, and she brushed them away impatiently. She'd become a right old softie the night Courtney arrived in the world.

'Just like her mother,' Nick sprawled out in the lounger beside them. He never stopped telling her how much he loved her and that he thought she was beautiful. They'd been married eighteen months and everything was wonderful. More than she'd ever hoped for.

Handing her the tissue box, he said to Courtney, 'I'd never have believed my wife had so many tears stored up until you came along, poppet.' He ran a finger lightly over his daughter's arm.

Leesa grinned and gazed around at the front lawn she'd spent the last year working to turn into a spectacular sight, even if she said so herself. The last two months of her pregnancy had seen a halt in progress as she struggled to get down on her knees or to wield a spade. But it was a work in progress, and being a garden, one that would never stop. 'I need to plant those tulip bulbs or I won't have any flowers in the spring.'

'There's a carton of bulbs waiting in the shed.'

'You bought some?'

'They're your favourites. Besides, we've filled the first spare bedroom, so I figured you'd want to get back to the garden before we start on the next room.'

She laughed. 'You hear that, Courtney? You're going to get a brother or sister but not for a while yet.' Courtney was barely three months old and they wanted to enjoy her before adding to the family again.

'We probably do need to slow down a bit. It's been a whirlwind since the night I proposed, hasn't it?'

'I like whirlwinds when you're in them.'

They'd bought the house by the beach within weeks of Nick coming to Gran's house to tell her he loved her. Then they had a beautiful wedding at her family's farm a few months later.

And out of the blue, Leesa found herself pregnant with Courtney days after they returned from their honeymoon in Fiji.

Life didn't get any better.

'Kevin phoned. He's bringing prawns and his

girlfriend for dinner. In that order,' Nick laughed. 'He mentioned Jodi and Brent might join us too.'

Okay, life could get better. Her heart swelled with love for all the people she cared about, and especially for these two, who she loved more than anything or anyone. Along the way she made the right choices and this was the reward. 'Love you two.'

Nick took his little girl and cradled her in one arm. Then he wrapped his other arm around the love of his life. 'Love you both back.'

He couldn't believe how happy he was. Every morning he got out of bed with a spring in his step. Every night he returned to their super king-sized bed with excitement in his veins to hold his wife against him.

Life was perfect. It wasn't glamorous or OTT, just idyllic and happy.

He'd come a long way from Adelaide, and he wasn't measuring that in kilometres. No, he'd found a life that involved family and a real home right here. All because of Leesa. She was the best thing to ever happen to him.

To think he'd only gone to that barbecue in Brisbane to give his mate and his mate's girlfriend some time to themselves. He might never have found love if not for that night.

He gazed around their property and love tugged

at him. Leesa had done a magnificent job of turning what had been a bald, dry area into stunning, colourful gardens and lots of green lawn for Baxter and Levi, another rescue dog, to play on. One day Courtney and any siblings that came along would play there too.

Yes, his heart was light and full of love. Life couldn't get any better.

* * * * *

If you enjoyed this story, check out these other great reads from Sue MacKay

Marriage Reunion with the Island Doc
Resisting the Pregnant Pediatrician
Fake Fiancée to Forever?
Brought Together by a Pup

All available now!

   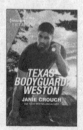